TREASURE
AT LURE LAKE

shari l. schwarz

TREASURE
AT LURE LAKE

SWEETWATER
BOOKS

An imprint of Cedar Fort, Inc.
Springville, Utah

ISBN 13: 978-1-4621-1790-1

Published by Sweetwater Books, an imprint of Cedar Fort, Inc.
2373 W. 700 S., Springville, UT 84663
Distributed by Cedar Fort, Inc., www.cedarfort.com

LIBRARY OF CONGRESS CATALOGING-IN-PUBLICATION DATA

Names: Schwarz, S. L., 1973- author.
Title: Treasure at Lure Lake / S.L. Schwarz.
Description: Springville, Utah : Sweetwater Books, an imprint of Cedar Fort, Inc., [2016] | ©2016 | Summary: Stumbling upon a treasure map connected to an old family secret, Bryce is determined to follow the clues to unearth both treasure and secret, even it means hiking in the wilderness with his bickering brother, Jack.
Identifiers: LCCN 2015045660 (print) | LCCN 2016004253 (ebook) | ISBN 9781462117901 (perfect bound : alk. paper) | ISBN 9781462126002 Subjects: | CYAC: Brothers--Fiction. | Survival--Fiction. | Wilderness areas--Fiction. | Secrets--Fiction. | LCGFT: Action and adventure fiction.
Classification: LCC PZ7.1.S3366 Tr 2016 (print) | LCC PZ7.1.S3366 (ebook) | DDC [Fic]--dc23
LC record available at http://lccn.loc.gov/2015045660

Cover design by Michelle May Ledezma
Cover design © 2016 by Cedar Fort, Inc.
Edited and typeset by Justin Greer

Printed in the United States of America

10 9 8 7 6 5 4 3 2 1

Printed on acid-free paper

To my dad,
who takes us
on the best adventures.

Chapter 1

Bryce

The promise of a treasure hunt led me into the darkness of Grandpa's barn. Out of the hot Colorado sun and away from my big brother, Jack, I could cool down and finally have some fun. I was tired of him making me play football. Being target practice for him wasn't my idea of a good time.

I trudged up the spiral staircase to the hayloft, mad at Jack for being the meanest brother in the entire universe.

At the top of the stairs, I opened boxes in Grandpa's storage area that I'd already gone through. I slid them out of my way, trying to avoid mouse poop and dead flies lying around. I slowly worked my way farther into the loft, digging through one box at a time.

Maybe I'd find something new, like last summer when I discovered Grandpa's old compound bow and arrows. He spent the rest of our vacation together teaching me how to shoot. It gave me something to do since Jack basically locked himself in the guest room for most of the week when I refused to play football with him.

Now, he was actually threatening to boycott our backpacking trip. If he didn't go, it would mess up the whole plan. It didn't even seem like we were brothers, and definitely not friends.

Mostly, I hoped to find Grandpa's rock climbing shoes and harness. I sure could use them on our backpacking trip next week. Dad used to take us climbing at the gym, back home in Atlanta. I couldn't wait to climb in the Rocky Mountains.

In a dusty box filled with yellow *National Geographic* magazines, I found a wooden slingshot. I shoved it into my back pocket to try out for later. I sneezed in the rising dust cloud and pulled out a pair of old aviator sunglasses. As I put them on my head, I noticed beads of sweat prickling my brow.

I needed a breeze or I wasn't going to last long, so I weaved my way through boxes and crates to open the window behind Grandma's antique sewing machine. On my way to the window, I tripped over a green plastic bin I'd never seen before.

Kneeling to open the bin, I flipped through a bunch of file folders filled with boring papers. I was about to close it up when I got to the last folder. But a thin wooden box stuck up out of the back. Weird that a box would be in a file folder.

I pulled it out and unlatched its golden clasp with a

click. Inside lay a pile of family photographs I'd never seen before. In the first one, Mom's hair was all curly and bleached blonde. I laughed at how different she looked. I couldn't believe she had overalls on. I was used to seeing her dressed up for work at the bank, her perfectly straight brown hair usually rolled into a bun.

Next to her in the picture, Dad's wavy brown hair stuck up in all directions like he'd just woken up. He had on an ugly, rust-colored, plaid jacket. I had seen it in the back of his closet at home when I was looking for a costume to wear for Halloween last year. I didn't realize he used to wear it for real.

But it wasn't only their clothes and hair and age that made them look different in the pictures. They actually looked happy.

Dad had his arms wrapped around Mom as she cradled two babies. There weren't any names on the back, so I guessed they were Jack and our cousin, Alex, who was about the same age.

In another picture, Mom and Dad sat on a tree branch gazing into each other's eyes like they were in love. I'd never seen them get that close before. It made me wonder what could have happened to make them so unhappy. These days they were so serious, working all the time. If they were home, they rarely talked to each other, like being together was too painful for them. Sometimes I was afraid they were going to get a divorce.

Over the last few months, I'd tried being extra good at home to help them get along better. I'd thought maybe it was working, but seeing the pictures made me realize I was wrong.

Underneath the pictures was a yellowed piece of paper.

As I unfolded it, my heart picked up speed with blazing excitement. I couldn't believe what I saw: a map of a house next to a river with a trail leading to a lake. Beside the lake was a tree, and beside the tree was an X.

My heart flashed. A treasure map? What could Grandpa be hiding?

And why would he be hiding it from me?

The metal staircase creaked and groaned under someone's weight, startling me from my thoughts.

"Bryce, you up there?" Grandpa yelled.

I jumped up, stuffing everything into my back pocket without thinking. I put the box back into the bin. Even though Grandpa told me to go ahead and snoop around anytime I wanted, I felt like I'd done something wrong, finding that box. Like it had been hidden away for a reason, not to be found, especially by me.

"Yeah," I shouted, stepping over an old-fashioned typewriter. "Coming!"

Grandpa appeared just as my toes reached the edge of the stairs. I held my breath to slow my pounding heartbeat, hoping he wouldn't notice my panic.

"How's it going?" Grandpa asked, peering at me from under the brim of his Rockies baseball cap.

"Uh . . . good. Just looking around." I tried to sound casual and stop my feet from shuffling.

"Hungry?" he asked, going back downstairs.

"Starving. What're we having?" I followed him to the farmhouse and gulped at the lump of guilt stuck in my throat.

"Tacos sound good?" he asked.

"Yeah. Sure."

Grandpa plucked the sunglasses off my head and laughed. "Did you find anything fun up there besides these?"

"Not really," I lied. "Just this." I pulled the slingshot out of my pocket and showed it to him on our way to the back porch. The lie just popped out of my mouth. I didn't know what I was so afraid of.

I'd never lied to Grandpa before.

I'd never stolen from him either.

"Oh, wow," said Grandpa, his brown eyes twinkling as he looked at the slingshot. "That brings back memories. You can have it if you want."

"Okay, sure." I figured if Grandpa gave me his

slingshot so easily, he probably wouldn't care about me having the map and the pictures for a while either. "I'll go wash my hands." I needed to figure out what to do. Maybe I could put them back after lunch. But I had to know what was up with the map.

After washing my hands, I ran upstairs with the pictures and map tucked under the front of my shirt. Over my shoulder, I yelled to Grandpa, "I'll be back down in a second."

In the bedroom, Jack was lying on his bed with his headphones on. I waved and waited for him to slide one off.

"Time for lunch," I announced, and in case Jack didn't believe me, I added, "Grandpa said so."

He rolled off the bed with a grunt and turned off his phone. I pretended to look for something in my backpack until he left so that I could hide the map and photos. I stashed them deep in the main pocket and raced back to the kitchen.

As I helped Grandpa carry plates into the dining room, I realized I wasn't very hungry anymore. I'd never kept anything from Grandpa before. He was probably my best friend in the whole world. But now that I'd betrayed him, I felt like the worst grandson he could ever have.

Chapter 2
Jack

Of course Dad canceled on us.

I don't know why I let it bug me so much, but it did. He said we'd have the best time: camping, hunting, fishing, climbing, hiking, four-wheeling.

And now?

Nothing.

Plus, Bryce made me even angrier trying to make excuses for Dad. Sure, I knew Dad's work was important. But now I was stuck going on the backpacking trip to play babysitter for Bryce.

Last night when Dad called, he made it very clear. "Yes, you still have to go, Jack. Help your grandpa with chores at the cabin. Keep an eye on Bryce. You know, stuff like that."

I should have known better than to get my hopes up that Dad would have actually shown up. When I asked him if I could talk to Mom, I heard them argue in the background. I pulled the phone away from my ear. I couldn't handle that.

Mom answered, and I begged her, "Please, don't make me go. I didn't even want to go in the first place. Why can't Grandpa just take Bryce? They don't need me."

"You have to go, Jack. Keep an eye on Bryce. Make sure he's safe . . . okay?"

Mom was always worried about Bryce. I could picture her nervously sliding her silver locket back and forth on its chain.

I sighed. Trying one last time to persuade her, I argued, "Grandpa will take care of him. They'll be fine."

"No, Jack, there are too many bad things that could happen out there. Three people are safer than two. I could never forgive myself if something happened to your little brother."

What about me, Mom? I thought. *What if something bad happens to me?* She was always protecting Bryce. Always babying him like he was made of gold and I was a cursed stepchild. I might think I was adopted if I didn't look exactly like my dad, with his wavy brown hair, bright blue eyes, and dimples. And Bryce had Mom's blue-gray eyes, Dad's brown hair, and one dimple on his right cheek.

"I'm sorry it's not going as planned," Mom continued. "Dad has some . . . well, things he needs to do, and maybe a last-minute business trip. Please try to make the best of it, sweetheart."

It was final. That was it. Dad never budged when he made a decision, unless it had to do with himself. He could get out of the backpacking trip, but there was no way I could.

After the phone call, Grandpa had knocked on the guest room door.

"Come in," I mumbled.

"Hey," he said and sat on the edge of my bed.

"Hey." I slid my headphones down around my neck.

"So . . . about your dad." He crossed his arms over his chest.

I shrugged, trying to blow it off like it wasn't a big deal.

"It's not your fault, you know."

I narrowed my eyes, wondering what Grandpa meant.

"Most likely, it's mine," he continued, rubbing his face with a weathered hand.

"What are you talking about?" I asked.

He hesitated, shrugged, and shook his head slightly. "Look. It's hard for him to come back here. Sometimes there are things, hard things, that keep people away. Since Grandma passed on, he's only been back here once. The last time we all hiked to the cabin. Remember?"

"Oh." I blinked, remembering back. That was a long time ago. I knew Dad and Grandpa didn't talk much. But I never thought about why Dad didn't visit his own father. Dad let us fly to Grandpa's every summer, so I assumed he at least trusted Grandpa. Or maybe he just wanted to get rid of us for a couple of weeks.

"So, we'll have a good time, right?" he asked, breaking in on my thoughts. "We'll still do everything we planned on. Sound good?"

I shrugged. I didn't have any other choice.

"And I'm counting on you to help me fix a few things at the cabin." He grinned as if that was supposed to make me feel better.

"Right, okay." I tried to smile back.

Grandpa hugged me from the side and left the room.

I checked my phone. Sophie had texted three times saying how excited she was that I got to go backpacking in the mountains. I started to answer her, but I couldn't think of anything to say that wouldn't sound lame, so I hit the delete key. I'd answer her later.

I plugged my headphones in, closed my eyes, and tried to fall asleep. But my anger, or maybe it was hurt, kept me tossing and turning all night long.

Chapter 3

Bryce

Three Days Later

After a three-hour, winding drive into the mountains, we finally made it to the trailhead. The one I'd been daydreaming about and planning for all year. I even had the topographical maps basically memorized and knew at least five different ways to start a fire. But, apparently, Jack still wasn't ready to go. He sat slouched in the back of Grandpa's Jeep, trying to text some girl he supposedly didn't have a crush on.

"Come on, Jack," I said, jumping out of the front. "There's no reception up here."

He lowered his dark eyebrows and kept jabbing at his cellphone.

"What do you need a girlfriend for anyway?" I muttered. He barely talked to anyone except for her, if texting counted as talking.

"We're just friends," he barked. "Leave me alone."

"You got a girlfriend," I teased, trying to get him out of the car. Any reaction would be better than his depressing mopiness.

Determined not to let him ruin my first minutes in the real wilderness, I reached into my backpack for my video camera, which was in the same pocket as the treasure map and pictures. I hadn't been able to find the right time to ask Grandpa about them. Glancing around to make sure no one was watching me, I slid them deeper into the pocket. My heart sped up, partly from excitement for our adventure and partly from the nervousness I'd felt since I first found the map.

The night before, I'd lain awake trying to figure out where the river, house, and lake on the map could be. It was nearly midnight when I realized how obvious it was. The house on the map was probably Grandpa's cabin. A river ran right by the cabin, and at the end of the trail was a lake. Lure Lake.

I just had to figure out the tree part of the map.

And the treasure part.

I flipped open my video camera and walked down the rocky bank to the edge of the swollen snowmelt river. I stood on a wobbly rock and videoed the water racing by. A huge tree floated past me followed by a whirlpool of branches and leaves—not a river to mess with.

I turned around and pointed my camera at the weathered trail sign.

I rewound in my head what I knew about bears. Make noise to keep them away. Roll into a ball if attacked. I'd had plenty of practice with Jack. A bear couldn't be much worse.

As if on cue, Jack grabbed me from behind. "Watch out for the bears, Bryce!" he yelled as I tried to push him off me. No use fighting him since he was twice my size, so I went limp like I did whenever he tackled me, causing us both to fall to the ground. He scrambled up and thumped me on the back as I stood.

"Cut it out!" I yelled, brushing dirt off my forearms and jeans.

He laughed and strode uphill to the Jeep. I didn't understand why he never took me seriously. It wasn't my fault I was younger or smaller than him. Why couldn't he just give me a break for once?

I refocused my camera, scanning the mountainside and panned to where aspen trees stood knee-deep in a flooded section of the river.

Grandpa limped down the bank and said, "What do you think, Bryce?"

"I can't believe we're finally here!" My voice cracked, startling me. Since I'd turned twelve, that happened at the worst times. I didn't want Grandpa to think I was afraid or anything.

"Ready to go?" he asked as he shotput a huge rock into the water. The *ker-sploosh* sounded a millisecond before cold drops splashed us.

"Absolutely!" I wiped water drops off my camera and then followed him to the Jeep where he had parked beside an old Ford pickup pulling a beat-up horse trailer.

Grandpa gathered me and Jack into his customary huddle, his arms across our shoulders, leaning close. We promised him to get along, be safe, and have a blast.

"Sorry again about your knee, Grandpa," Jack said.

"I'm fine, but next time we play basketball, watch out, 'cause *you'll* be the one with the swollen knee." Grandpa winked.

The day before, the three of us had been shooting hoops when Jack rammed into Grandpa on accident and laid him out flat. I was worried Grandpa had a concussion or worse. But it was his knee that took the hit. Luckily, after icing it all day, he was good enough to still go on our trip.

"Let's just enjoy ourselves out here and be safe," Grandpa said. "Got it?"

"Got it." Jack nodded, and I could have sworn he puffed out his chest.

"Get your packs on. Make sure you have your water bottles." Grandpa squeezed our shoulders. "I'll lock the Jeep. Then we can go."

Bending sideways, I pulled my twenty-eight-pound backpack onto my shoulder. At the same time, Jack turned toward the trail. His own backpack swung around and crashed into me. I teetered over a log and landed, *smack*, on my butt on a patch of prickly pear cacti.

"Oww! Jack!" The pain from the needles swirled together with Jack's laughter, making my eyes water.

"It's not my fault!" Jack said and leapt from one rock to another up the trail.

Angry, and determined like a steam engine, I yanked my backpack straps and hurried to catch up, pulling stray cactus needles from my jeans.

We finally were getting started, but it wasn't the way I'd planned on starting my epic adventure, that was for sure.

Chapter 4
Bryce

A few hours later, my anger toward Jack fizzled away as I focused on putting one foot in front of the other up the rocky trail. Grandpa whistled a folk tune behind me, which kept my legs moving to the beat even though I was dead tired. I wasn't used to the lack of oxygen in the high mountain air. Breathing hard, I glanced up at the bits of blue sky through the rattling aspen leaves, wishing for a strong breeze and deep shade.

Sometimes I complained to Mom and Dad on our hiking trips back home in Georgia, but the truth was, being out there gave me an open, soaring feeling. Like the top of a cage I'd been living in popped off, and I was flying free, like an eagle.

Even though I was happy to be on our hike, I felt awkward with Grandpa. It was bad enough that I was hiding something from him, but he was hiding something too. Now, only a thin piece of backpack material separated him from being able to see the map. I kept imagining it would jump out and hold up a neon sign saying, "Here I am! Your grandson stole me! Don't you know he's a thief?"

I shook away the guilty feelings and looked ahead for Jack. I hadn't seen his green backpack for a while, despite his promise that we'd stay together. No matter how hard I pumped my arms, I couldn't keep up with his long strides. I whistled sharply three times and yelled, "Jack! Stop!" Only my voice echoed back, bouncing off the canyon walls.

I hurried ahead as much as I could with the load I was hauling. My backpack banged against my back, egging me on. I shouted for Jack every few minutes but still couldn't see him. When I finally stopped to look back, I realized Grandpa, Jack, and I were totally separated from each other. Not smart. If anything happened to any one of us . . . well, I didn't want to think about what could happen out here. I had to get to Jack, slow him down. Grandpa would catch up with us soon.

Trudging along, I finally spotted something dark green through the trees—Jack's backpack. "Jack! Wait up. Grandpa's way back there."

When I finally reached him, Jack had climbed to the top of a huge boulder. He stood there with his arms crossed and stared down at me. I wanted to prove I could make it up too, but I struggled to reach high enough to a clear handhold. I slipped down over and over, scraping my forearms. I wouldn't give up, though. Not in front of him.

"Come on, you can do it," he said in a tone that was more demanding than encouraging.

I made it halfway but got stuck. I hated that everything was so much harder for me than for him. To make the situation even more embarassing, Jack yanked me up by my backpack like a sack of potatoes. I stood and steadied myself beside him, my neck and face heating with anger. "I could have made it on my own!"

"Right." Jack raised an eyebrow and sounded totally annoyed. "At this rate, we'll never make it to the cabin before dark." He gulped water from his canteen, handing me what was probably the backwash.

"We have the tent. We can camp anywhere along the way if we need to," I reminded him. I scowled into the canteen, not wanting to share with him. "Gross!"

"Take it or leave it." He set his lips in a thin line and shrugged his backpack on, clipping it around his chest and waist. Before I had a chance to rest and pull out my own water bottle, he took off again, picking his way down the backside of the boulder and around to the trail.

"Wait up!" I yelled, angry at him for storming off before Grandpa caught up, but I think he sped up instead.

A couple of minutes later, Jack veered toward the river. I leaned my backpack against a tree trunk, careful not to smash the purple wildflowers growing at its base.

"I'm going fishing while you have your rest time." Jack dug in his backpack for the tackle box and mumbled, "Don't want to be stuck babysitting you out here."

I folded my arms across my chest. "I don't need a babysitter."

"Good. Then try to keep up." Jack carried the pole past a clump of willowy bushes on his way to the river.

I hated it when he treated me like a little kid. He was such a jerk. Always making everything worse for me, as if it wasn't hard enough keeping up with someone almost three years older.

"You won't catch anything out there," I said, watching the water rush by.

Grandpa said I had an uncanny knack for smelling out a good fishing hole, and this wasn't one of them.

Jack set up the pole with a worm lure anyway and cast out over the gangly bushes. When he reeled the line in, it pulled tight. "See? I got one already."

But the line flung backward, sending a spray of water across my face, and tangled around a branch in front of us.

"It just got caught it in some rocks." I shook my head and wiped my eyes. "It's not gonna work. Let's go find Grandpa. His knee must be bugging him."

Jack ignored me and cast out again. I looked down the path, nervous about Grandpa being so far behind, but I knew better than to go off on my own again.

I stretched out on a flat boulder along the river to fill my water bottle. Instead of trying to find the water filter, I peeled off my sweaty T-shirt and folded it a few times over the mouth of the canteen, filtering and siphoning the water in.

Jack cast out a few more times but only snagged a stick.

He caught me smirking at him and growled, "You have a better idea?" He shoved the pole at me and jutted out his chin. "Be my guest."

"The best way to fish in a river is to get in there." But there was no way I'd get in that river. Not only was it freezing cold, I knew I wouldn't hold against its current for one second.

Jack shrugged. "Yeah, so?"

"So . . ." I pointed at the rapids. "Look at it."

Jack cocked his head. "I could stand in the middle of it if I wanted to. It's not that deep."

I didn't mean it as a dare, but of course Jack took it that way. "Don't be stupid," I warned him.

"I'll get in if you don't." He put his fists on his hips in defiance.

"Fine, go ahead. I'm not interested in dying today."

"I'm not gonna die." He looked at the river for a long moment before he kicked off his hiking shoes, pulled off each sock, and rolled his jeans up to his knees.

I wondered if he was having second thoughts. But then he walked without hesitation to the water's edge. I turned on my camera, ready to catch him in action, sure he was about to get wet.

"Stop pointing that thing at me," he said, but I zoomed in even closer.

That's when I caught a whiff of . . .

"Disgusting, Jack! Your feet stink!"

He rolled his eyes and stepped onto a rock sticking out of the river.

"Careful! Don't drop the pole," I yelled. It was the only one we brought, and it was Grandpa's. Nervously, I glanced downriver. Where was he anyway?

Jack lunged to another rock. Luckily, it held steady. As he reached back with the fishing pole and swiveled forward to cast the line out, it looked like he knew what he was doing for once. But just as smoothly, the rock slipped silently into the water and, in the blink of an eye, took Jack with it.

It all seemed to happen in slow motion. If only my

body could have reacted fast enough. In real time, only a split second lapsed as Jack splashed into the water and the fishing pole flew backward to the bank. In another second, Jack disappeared under the dark, surging water.

I scrambled after him, stumbling over rocks and branches. It seemed like forever before his head and arms popped up, flailing and spinning in the rapids.

Dodging a tree, I held my breath when he sank under again. It wasn't until he resurfaced that I yelled out, "Jack! Swim back!" The current tossed him like a fishing bobber with a trout struggling on its line. Suddenly, he jerked to one side and angled toward the bank.

I leapt over a log and pushed branches aside as he neared the bank, but it was deep and the water seemed to be boiling up though I knew it was cold. He was aiming toward a downed tree with roots dangling in the water.

"Jack! Grab the roots!" I yelled, but I wasn't sure he could even hear me.

He grappled at the roots just in time. He caught one and turned himself around so he was able to grab another one. I stretched out to him as far as I could. The current kept sweeping his legs out from under him, but he was able to wrap a root around one arm. He sputtered and coughed as the water piled into his face, already turning bluish.

I stretched out an inch farther, but I couldn't reach him without falling in. In a flash, I knew what I had to do.

"Hang on!" I yelled. "I'll be right back."

I ran back to our supplies, unlatched the climbing rope from my backpack, and raced to Jack. I tied a quick slipknot loop in one end of the rope and wound the other end around a tree. I threw the loop to Jack, but it got hung up on a bush near him. On my second throw, the rope hit Jack in the face and landed in the water, out of his reach. I pulled the rope back to shore. On the third-time's-a-charm time it landed, like a lasso, right over his head.

"Grab the rope," I shouted. "I'll pull you in!"

Jack hesitated, maybe unwilling to let go of his grip.

"You can do it," I urged him. "I'll hold you!"

I hoped I could hold him, but what if I couldn't?

Finally, he let go and grasped the rope. The force of his body weight jerked me forward much harder than I'd expected.

I didn't have enough strength to hold on.

Then, the rope went slack.

Chapter 5
Bryce

Jack crawled out of the water, hacking and sputtering.

"Yes!" I clapped, excited and relieved I'd been able to pull him out.

But he lay limp and ragged on the rocks and mud at the bank. Blood seeped from a gash on his leg.

"Are you okay?"

"I—I'm fr—free—zing," he chattered.

"Come on. You need to get dried off." I lifted his icy cold shoulders to help him stand.

The rope hung around his middle as we stumbled upriver to get his socks and shoes. He kept coughing and shuffled his feet as if lead weights were strapped to them.

I couldn't remember how quickly hypothermia could set in, but I didn't want to take any chances of him going into shock. I ran ahead to our supplies and clawed through our backpacks, flinging stuff everywhere in search of matches and the first aid kit. "Jack, didn't you pack the matches?"

He shrugged and peeled off his T-shirt. "I don't remember."

How could he not remember? Grandpa specifically asked him to pack them. "Probably too busy texting your girlfriend," I mumbled.

"What?" he asked.

I shook my head and found a bandage for the cut on his leg.

Where could the matches be? Maybe Grandpa had them. And where was Grandpa? What if he had been hurt too? How would I be able to take care of them both?

Looking down the trail, I yelled, "Grandpa!" in case he was nearby.

Jack dressed down to his boxers and stood, shivering and hugging himself. I tossed clothes to him. He put on a sweatshirt and dry boxers and unrolled his red sleeping bag. His hands were shaking so bad that I had to help him with the zipper. He slithered in until only his wet hair peeked out.

I couldn't believe what just happened. My brother could have been killed. Now, he needed to get warm. I raked my hands through the rest of his bag and came up with nothing to start a fire.

I forced myself to stop searching for the matches. I was just wasting time. I could make a fire other ways. Good thing, too, because the sun had gone down behind the mountains, which meant I couldn't use the magnifying glass method. There wasn't much time before it would get cool. I knew it could be freezing at night in the mountains, even in the summer, and there had been dark clouds coming in from the north all afternoon.

I turned in a circle, trying to figure out the best way to make a fire, when I noticed a piece of quartz rock poking out of the ground just a few feet away. In one of my adventure magazines, I'd read about how to use quartz to start sparks. I dug it up and found a few small boulders, side by side, about thirty yards uphill. They'd make the perfect backing for a fire pit.

I found just what I was looking for. Another rock, but one with green and orange patches of dry, flaky moss. Not like the kind of thick moss in Atlanta. I set my camera on a boulder and pressed record. Using my army knife, I scraped the moss into a small pile. Then I gathered a handful of dry grass and pine needles.

I flicked my knife against the quartz several times. Nothing happened. How long would this take? What if I couldn't start a fire? I'd never tried this method before.

Scraping harder and harder, I was about to give up when a flurry of sparks leapt into the moss, turning a very small part of it orange. It went out right away, but I kept at it. After two more tries the sparks took. I blew gently and fed the sparks one piece of dead grass at a time. I added a pine needle and kept blowing, feeling lightheaded. But I wouldn't give up. Jack needed a fire. With the temperature dropping, I figured we'd all need one soon.

"Yes! I got it," I yelled as a tiny flame flitted to life, and then another. The flames grew and spread, sending puffs of smoke into my nostrils. I coughed and fanned the fire. I added more debris, making sure it wouldn't go out.

"What are you yelling about?" Jack grumbled, hobbling toward me with his sleeping bag dragging behind him. He was still dressed only in his gray sweatshirt and boxers. His untied hiking shoes squelched as he walked to the fire.

"I made you a fire." How could he sound so ungrateful? I just saved his life.

"I'm fine," he grunted. Kicking off his shoes, he climbed in his sleeping bag and leaned against a rock close to the fire.

"Oh, okaaay." He sure didn't look fine to me, more like a cross between a white ghost and scraggly, wet rat.

Satisfaction welled within me when he scooted closer to the fire. He really did need the heat. And I was the one who'd been able to make it for him. The thought warmed me from the inside out, even if Jack was being a jerk about it.

I kept looking through the trees for Grandpa when, finally, I heard a familiar whistling.

"Grandpa! Up here!" I shouted. "Are you okay?"

He waved and limped uphill. One look at his round eyes and the set of his broad shoulders, and I knew we were in for it.

"What's all this?" He gestured at the small fire and Jack in his sleeping bag. "Setting up camp already?"

Jack and I exchanged glances, and since he was still shivering, I jumped in to explain. "Jack had a run-in with the river, and I'm trying to get him warmed up."

"What happened? Are you all right?" He crouched down to Jack.

Jack grimaced. "I'm fine. Just cold. I fell in, off a rock."

"Don't tell me you were showing off."

Jack sat up a bit, rubbed his head, and shrugged. "I was just trying to fish."

I was pretty sure Grandpa wasn't going to buy Jack's lie. It made me wonder if he had bought my lie about not finding anything interesting in the attic.

Grandpa shook his head. "It's not worth it to take chances up here. What would I tell your mom if . . ." Grandpa didn't finish his thought. "Are you sure you're okay? Did you hit your head?"

"Not hard."

"Let me look at your eyes. Close them for a minute." Grandpa checked to make sure his pupils dilated at the same time in case he had a concussion. "They look fine, but you let me know if you've got a headache or if you feel nauseous. Okay?"

Jack nodded. "I'm sorry. I shouldn't have gone near the river."

"It really is best if we stay together. I know you're itching to get to the cabin, but my knee was slowing me down. I had to rest for a while, and I had no idea where you guys were."

Jack looked down. I kind of felt bad for him. He'd been through a lot. But Grandpa was right. We had to stay together.

Grandpa cocked an eyebrow and inspected my fire. "You made this?"

I nodded, glad he was changing the subject. I kind of felt like it was my fault that Jack fell in since I gave him the idea of getting in the water.

"Nice job."

"Thanks. I'll clear a spot for the tent."

Grandpa nodded. "And I'll collect more firewood."

I sighed with relief that we weren't going to get in trouble. I hated the thought of Grandpa being upset with me. I watched him walk into the woods and tug a dry branch off a dead tree with a loud crack. How would I ever figure out how to tell him the truth about the map? I needed to do it soon.

"I'll just sleep here," said Jack.

"Against the rock? Under the tree branches?" I asked.

Jack grunted, closing his eyes. "Mmhmm. Just leave me alone."

"But what if a bird poops on you? Or it might rain. And what about wild animals at night?" I shivered thinking of all that could go wrong.

He shrugged and closed his eyes.

Nearby, I found a soft, grassy clearing that would make the perfect tent site. Camping under trees wasn't smart for several reasons, but for me, it was especially stupid, because I'd been pooped on by birds three times in my life.

Each time, the warm, slimy goo ran down my head or shoulder. Dad had told me it was good luck to be blessed by a bird, but I didn't think much of my good luck when I was pooped on the second and third times. I'd forfeit that kind of luck. I just needed the regular kind of luck now.

I threw aside a few pine cones and branches from the ground, hoping for at least one level area for us to sleep on. There would barely be enough room in the tent for all three of us to sleep side-by-side. Part of me hoped Jack wouldn't sleep in the tent just so me and Grandpa could stretch out a bit. It only took me a few minutes to set up the tent. I had slept in it lots of times in our backyard at home.

Overcoming the river, making a fire with my bare hands, and setting up camp made me feel strong, invincible. I imagined I was conquering the wilderness alone, using a rock to hammer the tent stakes into the ground. Not even Jack could stand in my way now.

But then, he disturbed my daydream with the loud *zzziiippp* of his sleeping bag. He got up and added a few sticks to the flames. I watched him out of the corner of my eye. I didn't want him ruining my fire.

Grandpa returned with an armful of wood when a sudden, eerie stillness came over the dimming forest. The birds stopped chirping as if they had all hunkered down to sleep at the same time. No more squirrels or chipmunks scampered around. The river seemed louder, now that the other sounds were gone.

We turned our heads toward a loud *crack* and a snuffling sound downhill. My heart raced, afraid of what could be out there. We looked at each other and then peered through the trees. There, past a clearing, a black shadow pawed through our backpacks. Jack stood up. His sleeping bag slunk down around his legs.

"Grandpa, look," I whispered urgently. I grabbed my camera from where it lay on the boulder and turned it on. Grandpa picked up a rock, and I bent to get one too. We sneaked closer a few feet. I could now see what I already knew it was—a black bear.

Even though a part of me was terrified, I was furious watching the bear tear into our food. I was even madder at myself for leaving our food out for so long. I knew better than that. I wanted to chase the bear away, but I didn't know if she would run away or turn on us.

"Shh," said Grandpa.

I stayed hidden behind a clump of trees. Grandpa licked his fingertips and raised them to check which way the wind was blowing. He gave me a thumbs-up. We were downwind from the bear.

A fearful excitement rippled through me at being closer to a dangerous wild animal than I'd ever been before. The bear tore open a bag of trail mix and spread it across the ground. "Aw, bummer," I said quietly. "That was my favorite." She licked it once but changed her mind and turned to nose through Jack's backpack, pulling out a bag of bagels. If we didn't act fast and scare the bear away, she'd end up eating our week's rations.

"Grandpa, what do we do?" I shivered and held up the rocks in my hands, wondering if we should use them.

He held one finger to his lips and shook his head.

Jack looked at the rocks in his hands, shrugged, and threw them with his quarterback precision. The rocks landed close to the bear, causing her to flinch and hop to one side. She looked up, but not directly at us, and continued nosing through the food. I wondered why Grandpa didn't scold Jack, but since he didn't, I threw my rock next, which didn't quite make the distance. The bear looked at the rock rolling on the ground and then up at us. She raised her head, sniffing the air. I pulled out my camera, hoping there was enough light to record something good enough to post to my YouTube channel. This might make me famous!

Jack gasped. "What's it doing?"

"Trying to smell us, I think."

"I don't want it to smell us." Jack hid behind a tree.

"And put that thing away." He pointed to my camera. "This is serious."

"No way. This is the best footage ever, and she's just trying to make sure we're not going to hurt her." My voice came out sounding much more confident than I felt, only because Grandpa was with us.

"How do you know, Einstein?" asked Jack.

"Because I've read the warning signs about bears at most every trail we've ever been to," I whispered.

"Boys, quiet down," warned Grandpa. "Let's just hope there aren't any cubs around."

That spooked me even more. I half-expected a couple of bear cubs to sneak up behind me.

The bear lowered her head, disinterested, and rooted around in the food again. I started to worry that she'd destroy the map and pictures. What if those were the only copies? How would I ever explain it all to Grandpa if they were ruined? I had a feeling this whole lying thing was not going to end well.

"We have to scare her off or we won't have any food left," I said, feeling desperate mostly about the pictures.

"It's worth a try," Grandpa said. He picked up a rock and a stick as long as I was tall.

I found a shorter one and planned to throw it spear-like at the bear. We crept closer until we were only about twenty feet away.

"On the count of three," said Grandpa.

We counted quietly, "One, two, three," and launched our spears through a clearing in the trees. Jack's stick hit the bear on its back, and mine hit a tree only halfway to her. The bear backed up and turned around as we launched our second attack. Jack threw more rocks and yelled like a warrior, driving the bear even farther away. Panting, I scrabbled at the ground, came up with a small pinecone, and threw it wildly as the bear kept going. Soon I couldn't distinguish her from the other shapes and shadows in the woods.

"Whoop!" Grandpa shouted into the air and high-fived me and Jack.

We stood there, squinting into the gray darkness, ready for another attack. My heart raced with excitement. *We did it!*

Now we needed at least enough time to clean up the mess and hang our supplies from a tree. I should have that done in the first place. I'd been so distracted with saving Jack and making a fire for him that I forgot about the basics of surviving out here. Stupid. I wouldn't let it happen again.

"Come on," Grandpa said. "Let's clean up and hang everything before she changes her mind."

We scraped together the small amount of food that was intact and packed it along with the rest of our supplies, aside from what we'd need for the night. I found an unopened bag of pretzels and power bars the bear had missed. I saved them for dinner and checked for the map and pictures. When I found them, still in the bottom of the main pocket of my backpack and unharmed, I sighed with relief.

"What is it?" Grandpa asked while stringing the climbing rope through his backpack straps.

"What is what?" I jerked my head toward him, afraid he knew what I was doing.

"Such a deep sigh. Are you looking for something?"

Guilt lobbed in my stomach again. "Oh. Uh . . . no. I'm

fine." I zipped my backpack and stood. What if Grandpa was getting suspicious? I had to find a way to tell him the truth, but the longer I waited, the bigger my crime got.

Jack tried throwing the rope over a high tree branch and missed.

"They have to be at least ten feet off the ground and ten feet from any other tree trunk to be safe from the bear." I hoped I'd distracted Grandpa from being suspicious.

Jack whispered under his breath, "I know. Stop being so bossy."

"I just don't want the bear to come back." My skin crawled, wondering if she was watching us, waiting to sneak up when we weren't looking.

Jack finally got the backpacks up and tied a series of knots around a low branch to anchor them in the tree. Looking uphill, I searched for the glow of the fire. Hopefully it hadn't gone out. I didn't want to stumble onto the bear or her cubs if they were out there.

If anything, the fire gave me hope. Hope that we would survive the night and make it through our crazy adventure alive and in one piece.

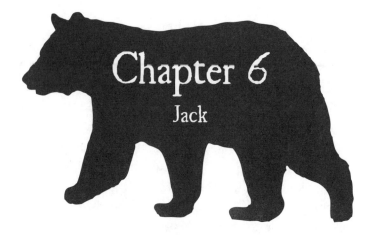

Chapter 6
Jack

I f the bear was following us, watching us stumble to the barely existent fire, I didn't want to know about it. But I made sure my army knife was in my pocket, ready for anything.

"Let's get more wood on our way up," suggested Grandpa, looking over his shoulder. He must have been worried too.

The rough bark of the pine branches scraped me as I loaded my arms full. We added a few twigs to the fire. Bryce blew on the coals, starting the flames again. As I spread my fingers in front of the fire, I noticed they were still shaking from falling in the stupid river.

I couldn't believe that rock slipped out from under me. I almost drowned to death. What a way to go. And that bear? Almost destroying our camp? Things were not going as planned. I had hoped to be settled at the cabin, playing catch with Grandpa or on my iPhone by now, and maybe even having reception up higher on the mountain. I wondered if Sophie had texted me again. She'd been telling me to cheer up and have a good time. But I took my frustration out on her and told her to stop sounding like my mom. Now I felt bad and hoped she wasn't hurt and mad at me.

I sat on a stump by the fire and stretched out my legs. I didn't realize how banged up they were from the river dragging me over boulders. Luckily, I'd hit that big one feet first and rebounded off it back toward the bank.

Bryce handed me a power bar. "Here," he said. "So much for that trout dinner, huh?"

"Not funny." I ripped open the wrapper.

Bryce knelt by the fire. Talking with his mouth full, he said, "I can't believe the nerve of that bear."

That was one thing we could agree on. "I was almost mad enough to tackle it," I grumbled, imagining wrestling with a black bear. I ate my power bar in three bites. Not much of a dinner, but everything else was either spoiled by the bear or hanging exactly ten feet up in the air. I pulled my knees toward me and discovered a goose egg on my shin where I'd gotten cut.

Grandpa came out of the tent, and Bryce handed me a bag of pretzels. "Want some?"

"Sure. I was thinking . . . maybe we should take shifts throughout the night. Watch for the bear and keep the fire going."

While Bryce annoyingly munched on his pretzels, he said, "Yeah, that's probably a good idea. What do you think, Grandpa?"

"Sounds good to me. The fire should keep the bear away too." He scooped a handful of pretzels and sat between us.

I crawled into my sleeping bag. "I'll take the first shift since I never can fall asleep on camping trips anyway. If I get too sleepy, who should I wake first?"

"I'll take second shift," said Grandpa. "But wake me at any time if something's wrong."

Later, after Grandpa and Bryce zipped themselves into their cocoon of a tent, I stared into the flames and smacked a mosquito buzzing around my head. I decided to carve a stick to pass the time.

All I could hear was the roar of the river and the scraping of my knife on a chunk of wood. But as I sat there, I started to hear other sounds. The wind shifted through the trees and an owl hooted.

Later, coyotes howled in the distance. I tensed, looking up from my stick into the dread, black night. I couldn't see anything past the circle of light around the fire. But I knew whatever was out there could definitely see me.

I hated the first night of camping trips. I'd never fall asleep until dawn. If only I could listen to music on my iPhone to pass the time, but it was tied up in the tree. I fidgeted to find the most comfortable spot on the hard, lumpy ground and pulled my sleeping bag up to my chin as the night turned cold.

Thick, damp air settled in. The smell of dirt and smoke swirled around me as sparks shot into the inklike darkness. I folded my poncho to use as a pillow and situated my back against a boulder. That way, I could look downhill to watch for the bear, and it couldn't sneak up behind me.

Much later, a foggy drizzle filled the air. I spread my poncho over my sleeping bag to keep from getting wet, but the frost cut through all the layers. My nose and cheeks felt frozen.

I couldn't wait till we got to the cabin, warm and safe. Hopefully, Bryce would stop bugging me with his stupid camera and stop acting like he knew everything.

It was just my luck that he'd go all superhero on me, pull me out of the river, and make a fire I couldn't resist. I could have gotten out by myself.

He probably thought I owed him one.

I twisted deeper into my sleeping bag.

I just wanted to be left alone.

Some time later, something jerked me out of a hazy sleep. I peeked out of my sleeping bag and listened carefully. All I could hear was the white noise of the river. I couldn't see a thing. The fire must have gone out. Terror gripped me, wondering how long I'd been out.

I couldn't feel my toes, and something cold was falling on my face, pelting me. Ice? Could there really be an ice storm in June?

I rubbed my nose to warm it up. That's when I noticed an awful smell. Like I was at the petting zoo, or worse. I pulled my head under the poncho and kept listening, wondering what had woken me up.

Crack! There it was, loud and close, the sound of something shuffling around me and smashing above me. I couldn't help but flinch. I hoped whatever it was wouldn't notice me.

Something hard rubbed against my side. I wanted to scream, but I felt paralyzed. The stench in the air made my stomach roll. Heavy breathing puffed close to my ear.

I didn't want it to bite my head off, so I slowly rolled over and peered out of the poncho. A slight glow from the clouded moon highlighted a huge, dark mass hovering above me. It was about to attack!

It moved closer again and nudged me, poking my ribs. I closed my eyes and held my breath, sure I was about to be mauled.

I'm only fourteen. I can't die now. What will happen to me if I die? Will I just stop being? Be nothing? Turn into dust? If my life is only worth a bottle full of dirt, what is the point of anything? All these thoughts raced through my mind in an instant.

"Please go away, please go away," I whispered. But it didn't. It wouldn't. It poked me in the thigh next, enough that it hurt, adding to my bruises from the river. I was going to die. For the second time in one day, I was sure of it. It made me wonder how many times a person could evade death in one day. This couldn't be happening to me.

The animal nudged me again and grunted. I rolled closer to the boulder. My life flashed before me in stop-motion scenes, reminding me of some of the dumb things I'd done lately: skipping school, sneaking out to a party one night. Those things didn't seem as exciting or important anymore. I made a promise I'd be better if I could only live.

I lay as still as a statue, barely breathing, until the shuffling retreated. I could see its shape—long legs, a bulky body. Branches above it. Wait, how did those branches get up there? The branches moved closer to me. That's when I realized they weren't branches at all, but antlers.

Too big to be a deer, it had to be an elk. Not a bear.

I let my breath out slowly, somewhat relieved, but I knew an elk could kill too, if it gored me. Bryce showed me that on YouTube once. When it stepped away, I scrambled behind the boulders. Maybe I would die from the cold tonight, but not from a bear or the elk if I could help it.

It took a few minutes before I could move again, but all the trouble I'd gotten into in the past year haunted me. I knew I disappointed Mom and Dad. Probably on a daily basis. It felt like my entire existence disappointed them. Mom rarely looked me straight in the eyes, and when she did, I only saw sadness there. Bryce was the one who made her happy. She always bragged on him and gave him all the attention. I didn't know what I had done to cause it.

And I didn't know what to do to stop it.

And now, I might never have the chance to tell her I was sorry for being such a pain or to give her a big hug and let her know I'd try harder. Maybe there was some way I could make her and Dad proud of me. Maybe Mom wouldn't be so sad if I could remember to take out the trash or clean her car for her. Stuff she was always muttering about.

I crawled out of my sleeping bag, put it over my head and shoulders, and shoved on my shoes. I stumbled to the tent to wake Grandpa. I sure hoped the three of us could fit in there. The rain really had turned to ice, coating the tent. I was shivering again.

I unzipped the tent, startling Bryce. He sat straight up, his head sliding across the top of the tent ceiling.

"What is it?" he asked, his voice thick and slow, while Grandpa snored deeply.

"Nothing. It's sleeting. I'm gonna sleep in here."

Bryce rolled over as I squeezed in between him and Grandpa. I didn't want to be on the outside, against the thin tent wall as the only protection between me and the dark night.

"What about the bear?"

"I don't think the bear is prowling around in this weather," I said, hopeful. "Plus, I ran into an elk."

"You what?"

I zipped up my sleeping bag and sighed. "I'll tell you about it in the morning. Let's just say, if an elk's hanging out nearby, I'm sure the bear isn't."

"Yeah, okay, that's probably true." Bryce yawned.

"Night."

"Mmhmm," he mumbled.

I covered my head with my sweatshirt, hoping for more sleep. But whether I got any more or not didn't matter. At least I was safe in the tent with Bryce and Grandpa.

Chapter 7

Jack

In the morning, the birds' shrill chatter broke through my restless sleep. The piercing sun lit up our orange tent. I slid deeper into my sleeping bag to avoid the light when a backache shot up my neck and into my head. But the ache in my stomach eclipsed all my other senses. I'd hardly eaten anything since we started out yesterday.

I unfolded my stiff, cold muscles and rubbed my eyes, thankful we survived the night. Grandpa was still asleep beside me, but Bryce was gone. Wondering where he was, I sat up with my sleeping bag still on and leaned forward to open the tent flap. I peeked out. The spotless blue sky in one direction was scuffed by dark, hazy clouds in the south. Everything—the ground, the pine needles, the outside of the tent—was covered with a thin layer of shimmery, lacy ice. I pulled on my hiking shoes, grabbed my water bottle, and flipped up my hood. On the way to the river, I used a clump of aspen leaves for toilet paper and squatted behind a bush. Survival 101.

I called out, "Bryce!"

His familiar three sharp whistles answered me through the trees in the direction of our backpacks. He must have gotten our stuff down from the tree, because he was carrying his backpack over one shoulder.

"Are you okay?" Bryce asked.

I nodded and met him at the fire pit.

"So what happened last night? You said something about an elk."

"Yeah, it nudged me a few times with its antlers. Scared me half to death. At first, I thought it was the bear, but then I saw its outline." I looked down to where Bryce pointed at elk tracks in the dirt.

"It didn't hurt you?"

"Not really. I lay there as still as I could. I couldn't believe I had fallen asleep. I was—"

"Wait," Bryce interrupted me. "You fell asleep?"

"Uh, yeah." I turned to face him as he glared at me. What did I do wrong now?

"How could you? You were supposed to keep watch." His eyes widened as he gestured wildly. "We trusted you."

I didn't understand why was he was getting so worked up. "Sorry!" I said. "I didn't mean to. I wasn't asleep long." I really had no idea how long I'd been sleeping, but Bryce was overreacting as usual.

"That doesn't matter! You could have gotten us killed,

Jack. What if it had been the bear? Or something worse?"

"Worse?" I asked. "What could be worse?"

"A mountain lion!" he yelled.

"I said I'm sorry." I turned away from him.

"You don't sound like you're sorry." Bryce reached out and grabbed my arm, turning me to face him.

I clenched my fists and almost punched him. Shaking him off, I said, "Look. What do you want me to do about it? It's over and done with, and we're both fine."

"Luckily. But how am I supposed to trust you next time?"

"Bryce, let it go. You sound like Mom." He was such a worrier. I didn't know if I'd be able to stand the rest of the trip with him if he was going to act that way.

"I'm serious, Jack. What if we're not so lucky next time?" He sounded like he was going to cry. Seriously? He was such a baby.

"You and your luck," I challenged. "It's not always about luck, you know. Sometimes things just are the way they are. Or they happen the way they happen. No luck involved. That's life. Let it go."

I had to walk away or I was going to pummel him. How could he be so judgmental? I bet he would've fallen asleep too if he'd been keeping watch.

I stomped away to untangle the backpacks from high in the trees, hoping there was more food left than I'd thought. Bryce followed me, of course, like a puppy dog. I wished he'd just leave me alone.

I ignored him and let my backpack down, winding the rope around my hand and elbow.

There wasn't much food left in my backpack. Just some ketchup, mustard, spaghetti sauce, and a jar of peanut butter. There was more in Bryce's: a pouch of tuna fish, a package of pasta, and another box of power bars.

Bryce yelled, "Hey! Get out of my backpack!"

"I'm just trying to see what's left."

He shoved me away. "I'll do it."

"Watch it!" Why was he getting so pushy? I decided to let it go and checked Grandpa's backpack which, luckily, was mostly untouched.

Grandpa came out of the tent and said, "Morning, guys! That was a cold one, huh?"

I nodded. "Freezing."

"Grandpa, guess what?" started Bryce.

I could tell he was about to tattle on me for falling asleep. I shot him a narrow look, hoping to stop him.

"What is it?" asked Grandpa, walking toward us.

"Jack saw an elk last night while he was keeping watch and . . . and he almost died." Bryce trailed off. "And we're figuring out breakfast." He held up a half-chewed bag of bagels.

"What happened?" Grandpa ran his hands through his graying hair. "Why didn't you wake me?"

I shook my head. "I didn't want to make a noise. I thought it was the bear at first . . . I totally thought I was a goner."

Bryce shrugged. "Just would've meant more food for us."

I glared at him. As usual, I didn't think he was funny at all. I really had been freaked out. And what if I had died?

I glanced up at a hawk soaring above us. It made me wonder if my life would only mean the difference between Bryce being hungry or not. What would really happen if I was just gone. There had to be more to life than my meaningless existence. More than something that could be snuffed out in an instant.

As if reading my thoughts, Grandpa frowned at Bryce and said, "It would have meant a whole lot of sorrow for a whole lot of people."

I sighed. "When I realized it was an elk, I knew not to mess with it. Eventually, it walked away."

"How close did it get to you?" Grandpa asked.

I didn't want to worry him. I hoped he wouldn't freak out. "It actually poked me a few times." I pointed to my side and my hip.

His eyes grew wide.

"But I'm okay," I added quickly. "I'm fine."

"Well, thank heavens. Don't know what I'd do if something happened to you, Jack." He held his arms out for a hug. "No more close calls, okay?"

I closed the distance between us. I hadn't had a big bear hug in a long time. I hated to admit it, but it felt good, like Grandpa's arms could hold me up no matter what happened.

Bryce interrupted us, shaking the mangled bag of bagels. "Anyone want breakfast?"

"That's gross!" I shook my head, wondering how much bear slobber was on them.

Next, he held up a gallon-sized Ziploc bag of Froot Loops. "Score!" he said, looking in his backpack. "Aw, darn. The powdered milk spilled all over everything."

"Well, at least Froot Loops taste good any which way," said Grandpa. "So, Jack, why didn't you wake me last night?"

I shrugged. "It was too cold for anyone to be out there

in the ice storm, and with the elk near us I figured we were safe from the bear. Plus, you were snoring away."

He smirked. "Sorry 'bout that. That was your grandma's pet peeve. Hope I didn't keep you awake."

I shook my head. If anything kept me awake, it was fear.

"Let's have some cereal before we clean up and head to the cabin," Grandpa said. "We'll be able to lay everything out when we get there and see what we have to work with."

"Fine by me."

We scooped handfuls of dry Froot Loops and used our pocketknives to eat peanut butter straight out of the jar. Mom would not have approved of our double-dipping at all, but I'm pretty sure peanut butter had never tasted so good to me before.

After making sure the fire was totally out, we hiked along the river again. I kept searching the shadows in the trees for the bear. I had a feeling it was watching us, waiting to snatch the rest of our food—and hopefully nothing more.

Chapter 8

Bryce

Jack led the way north, breaking out ahead of me and Grandpa again. After about an hour of hiking, my legs and lungs burned with exhaustion, making me feel like I'd run a marathon after only a short time.

"Jack, wait up! I need a break," I called. Why couldn't he slow down for once?

When I finally caught up, he was sitting on a rock beside the river. A bunch of dandelions poked up out of a grassy patch.

Still mad at him for leaving us exposed in the night, I yanked one up and stuck out my tongue to taste-test it. It tasted green, bitter, and flowery, just like a dandelion smells. I dropped my backpack and sat on another rock.

"Want one?" I asked with the stem hanging from my mouth.

He scowled and crossed his arms over his chest. "Are you kidding? You think I'd eat that?"

"Sure, why not? It's food." I munched on it to prove how daring I was.

"Forget it. I'm not that desperate."

"Well, you will be if we run out of food before Thursday," I said, chewing with my mouth open to annoy him.

"We'll be fine." He put on his backpack and hiked off without another word. Even though I wanted to rest longer, I followed him. There wasn't any good reason to stick around and waste time. Grandpa wasn't too far behind. I could see him coming around a bend in the trail.

A few minutes later, voices boomed ahead of us. Two men were hiking down the trail.

The first guy, tall and lanky with a full beard, passed us. "How's it going?" His voice rumbled like thunder.

"Great." Jack nodded.

The second man had his arm bandaged in what looked like strips of a T-shirt. He pulled a donkey behind him. "You boys all right?"

"Yep," said Jack, narrowing his eyes. The donkey was loaded down with two rifles sticking out of the bulging saddlebags.

"You two all alone?"

"Nope," Jack answered. "Our grandpa and dad are back there."

I blinked at Jack's lie even though it was partly true. Plus, Dad should have been there with us. Which made me wonder why Dad never was able to make it when Grandpa was involved. The tension between them was too thick to ignore. Actually, the tension between Dad and Mom was pretty bad too. And between Dad and Jack. I had hoped our trip would help everyone get along better. I hated always feeling like I had to be the go-between in my family.

The men looked down the trail and back at us, probably wondering if Jack was telling the truth. Grandpa was just a little bit farther.

The shorter man was stocky and bald—the opposite of his friend, whose strands of greasy hair hung beneath his gray fisherman's hat. Green canvas backpacks reached over their heads, and the men looked really dirty, like they'd been out there for a while. What if they were up to no good? What if they were after the treasure?

"Alrighty then, have a good hike," the tall man said and turned down the trail.

"They look like trouble," Jack whispered when they were gone.

"Why do you say that?"

"I don't know. They just do." Jack glanced back a few times as we waited for Grandpa while he chatted with the men.

"What is it, Jack?" He was freaking me out.

He wiped his nose and said, "They just don't look like typical hikers."

"Yeah, but we probably don't either." If anything, we were the ones not to be trusted. Jack had flat-out lied to them. But still, I wondered if they knew about the treasure. What if they'd gotten there before me?

Jack shrugged and waved to Grandpa coming up the

trail. "They look like squatters or poachers."

"Grandpa, do you think those guys are up to something?"

"Those guys?" He jerked his thumb over his shoulder.

"Yeah, Jack thinks they look suspicious."

Grandpa shook his head. "Nah. They seemed nice enough to me. Said they were concerned when they saw two young boys out here alone."

Jack scowled and mumbled. "Fourteen's not that young."

Grandpa stifled a chuckle. "Don't worry about them. Let's keep going." He swept his hands, low through the air, like he was herding us.

I took one last look behind me and sighed. The men were out of sight, but my worry was only increasing. I hoped we wouldn't see them again.

Chapter 9
Bryce

I had my camera ready when I spotted the cabin. Memories flashed through my mind: roasting marshmallows over a campfire, collecting flowers for Mom, fishing at the lake with Grandpa. Good flashbacks filled my chest with a huge, relieved sigh. "We made it, Grandpa!"

"Yeehaw!" he shouted, causing a couple of birds to scatter from a nearby bush. "Do you remember the last time you were here?"

"Yep. A little." It had been about five or six years ago. Ever since then, Mom and Dad had been sending us out alone to Grandpa's for a week or two during summer vacation. On the flights from Atlanta to Denver and back, the stewardesses used to give us lots of attention, like extra snacks and drinks and airplane prizes. They didn't seem to notice us anymore since Jack was as tall as a full-grown man.

Adrenaline swirled through me as I veered off the trail. The memories of being here with Mom and Dad before reminded me about the pictures and map. Now I'd have to find a way to get to the lake and the treasure without Grandpa suspecting anything. Not like I was going to steal whatever was there. I was just curious.

Maybe Jack would help me if I told him about it. He liked a good mystery. And he was good at figuring things out. But he'd probably tell on me, and Grandpa would never trust me again. So, I was back to square one.

Suddenly, my adrenaline turned into mushy guilt glopping to the bottom of my stomach. I hated keeping a secret from Grandpa. Maybe I could still tell him. Act like I'd forgotten about it. Grandpa caught up with me in the tangled underbrush, and I buried the thought by focusing on the cabin.

It sat back from the river amid an aspen grove. Overgrown bushes partially hid it from view. No wonder Jack had hiked right on past it. I whistled to get his attention. "Jack! Here it is!"

He turned and threw his arms in the air as if exasperated. It wasn't my fault he hadn't seen it. Serves him right for racing ahead.

Grandpa's smile spread from cheek to cheek. "I inherited it from my father, you know. He built it after he moved to Colorado in the 1940s and hauled the tools and materials up with his donkey. Can you imagine?"

"That must have taken forever," I said as we walked through the trees to the cabin's front porch.

"He chopped down trees right here off his own land." Grandpa set his backpack down and took the cabin key out as Jack leapt up to the porch.

"I *thought* this was it . . . ," Jack said lamely, probably embarrassed that he'd hiked right on past it.

"Glad you could join us," Grandpa joked and started to unlock the door. "Hmm. That's strange. It's not locked." The door creaked on its thick metal hinges when he pushed it open. Beams of dusty light shot into the dark, earthy-smelling room.

I stepped in, and that's when I noticed the broken window. The dark green curtain fluttered in the breeze. I swung my camera around to catch the damage in real time. "Grandpa, look what happened!"

I opened the curtains, careful not to step on the broken glass. I wondered if those men on the trail had broken in. It must have been them. A tingling spread across my arms and back, prickling the hairs on my neck at the thought of intruders.

"Oh, no. This happened once before," Grandpa said, taking off his baseball cap and wiping the sweat from his forehead. He and Jack were still outside, inspecting the window.

"Maybe those guys broke in," said Jack.

"They better not come back." I opened the curtains of another window to let the light chase out the creepy feelings I had.

"There aren't any leaves . . . or any sign of rain coming in," said Jack. "It had to have happened recently. And look! There's dried blood here." He squatted down near the broken glass.

I stood beside him, eyeing the blood. "What if it was an animal?"

"If it was, there'd be something else, like hair stuck in the glass—or feathers if it was a bird."

"Look who's the big detective," I teased. I knew he wanted to be a policeman or detective someday, and really, I wished I could be as good as him at figuring out stuff like that.

Jack ignored me and went to the pantry at the far wall of the cabin near a wooden dry sink. "There's hardly any food in here. I bet they broke in and stole it." He banged the doors shut and spun around, looking for something else.

"What is it?" I stood in the doorway, gaping at him.

Jack shook his head and narrowed his deep-set blue eyes. "I wonder what else they took."

"Let's not jump to conclusions," cautioned Grandpa. "It could have been broken from any number of things."

I followed Jack to the river-rock fireplace.

"Would you have left coals in the fireplace the last time you were here, Grandpa?" Jack asked.

Grandpa strode to the fireplace and sighed. "You might be right after all. I've had a couple of break-ins before, but it's usually because someone was in desperate need of shelter. Those guys probably had a good reason and didn't mean any harm. They did look like they were in rough shape."

My grumbling stomach led me to the pantry to see what the men had left. On the middle shelf were two cans of baked beans, a can of Spam, sweet corn, chili with meat, and a box of chocolate chip granola bars. "At least they didn't take everything."

Grandpa looked through the shelves full of green camping plates, bowls, mugs, pots and pans, and other kitchen supplies. A single packet of hot cocoa mix and a bag of stale marshmallows were on the top shelf, along with salt, pepper, and small bottles of spices.

"It doesn't look like they took too much," Grandpa said. "I'm not even sure if they ate any food. I don't really remember what I left up here last time."

"Well, I'm starving." Jack reached over my head and gathered the food. "What should we have for lunch?"

I swatted at his arm and ducked out from underneath him. I hated being reminded of how much taller he was than me. Hopefully I'd get my growth spurt soon. The last time Mom marked my height on the laundry room doorjamb at home, she'd assured me it would happen when it was meant to.

I just hoped it would decide this summer was the right time.

"Go ahead and dig into the cans with meat, since they probably need to be eaten first," said Grandpa.

Jack opened the container of Spam and asked Grandpa, "Want some?"

He held up his hand. "Can't stand the stuff. You go ahead."

I held up a knife and cut a line down the middle of the Spam using Mom's tried-and-true method she called "The Rule of Halves," where the first person cuts the food in half and the second person gets to choose which half they want. If I didn't do that, Jack would hog the biggest piece. He might be bigger than me, but he was probably done growing. I was the one who needed the extra calories to put on weight.

Grandpa opened the corn and chili with his knife. We ate the food cold, straight out of the cans. It didn't taste so bad after the first couple of bites. After we devoured it all, we unpacked our backpacks and spread all our food on the wooden kitchen table. Grandpa had Hershey's bars, graham crackers, and marshmallows, half a dozen eggs in a hard plastic container, lemonade mix, beef jerky, and hard salami. At least we had enough to keep us from starving.

But too soon, we were done eating, and I slumped at the table. With a half-full stomach, my expectation for a pantry full of food left me feeling emptier than ever. "There's not as much food here as I'd hoped." I sure missed Mom and wished for a big, fat steak-and-baked-potato dinner that she cooked for my birthday every year.

"Well," said Grandpa, "here's your chance to make those snare traps like you've been wanting to, right?" He patted my back. "I'll fix the window while you two figure out what you want to do for food. Whatever you do, though, don't go wandering off without telling me."

"And we can hike to the lake tomorrow to fish, right?" I tried to sound just the right amount of excited for a kid who loves to fish but is lying about a treasure hunt he has to go on.

I pushed away from the kitchen table and shuffled to the one bedroom in the cabin. Under the window, on a simple writing desk, sat a small blue vase. Mom had used it for wildflowers when we were all here last time. I remembered thinking it would cheer her up after she and Dad had gotten in a fight and she had run into the bedroom, crying.

As I plopped onto the double bed against the opposite wall, a cloud of dust rose around me.

"Boys." Grandpa walked into the bedroom with Jack behind him. "We've got some work to do before we can relax. Jack, you filter water and fill the water bottles at the stream. I'll collect firewood, and Bryce, you set a couple traps out there. See what you can catch us for dinner."

It was the chance I'd been looking forward to. Surviving like an explorer in the olden days. But now that I had to make and set traps, without a bunch of food waiting for us in the pantry as backup, I was more worried than excited.

My traps didn't always work.

Chapter 10

Bryce

A stream wound its way down the mountainside and joined the river at a clear, pooled area where it spilled over several stair-stepped rocks, purifying the water naturally. Jack knelt beside the stream, pumping the water filter. One of my least favorite chores. It took so much time and strength to pump the filter that my hands would turn numb from the freezing water. Jack was much faster at it than me.

I had my camera in my hand as I wandered around, looking for just the right kind of sticks for different parts of my traps. I kept my eye out for any squirrels or chipmunks running around, or tracks that would signal a likely spot to catch an animal.

Uphill, I knelt to build a trap near a rocky area. Striped chipmunks dashed in and out of the rocks. I drove two forked sticks into the ground about eight inches apart. Placing a third stick on top, through the forks, I secured them with pieces of fishing line. I hung a wire noose from the stick. A few well-placed rocks made the trap sturdier. Using more rocks, I created an alleyway to hopefully guide an animal toward the noose. I'd tried that method a few times back home and had caught a couple of rabbits with it.

I set another trap by the stream, where animal tracks crisscrossed each other. I hoped for good luck—the real kind, not the bird poop kind.

I kept an eye out for plants or berries we could eat. I'd read a little about mushrooms, but there were so many different kinds that I knew better than to touch them. I'd leave that job for Grandpa. He knew which ones were safe to eat.

I kicked at a pinecone. As it tumbled over the bumpy ground, it reminded me of how Mom sometimes used pine nuts at home. But the ones she bought from the store were shelled already.

When I bent to pick it up, something small and red in the shade of a bush caught my eye. I reached down and brushed my hand across a bunch of green leaves. Beneath them were tiny white flowers and some berries. I picked one, wondering if it was edible. Although it was small, it was most definitely a strawberry, much smaller than the kind from the grocery store or the ones Mom grew in her garden. I popped it in my mouth. The intense sweetness melted across my tongue. I'd never tasted anything so amazing! I collected every single one I could find, eating them on the spot like a pirate hoarding a treasure.

"What are you doing?" Jack walked up to me from the stream.

"Look!" I handed him the last one. "Strawberries."

He grimaced at it as if I was going to poison him.

"Eat it."

"No. You, first."

"I already ate a bunch."

He held it up to his eye. What was he doing? Looking for bugs? He smelled it and threw it into his mouth. He chewed and paused before he *Mm-mmmed*, his eyes growing wide with surprise.

"Good, huh?" I asked.

He nodded. "Are there more?"

"Umm . . ." I squatted down but couldn't find any more. "I guess I ate them all."

"All of them?" Jack asked accusingly.

"At least I saved you one." I couldn't have Jack being upset with me. He'd make my life miserable if he was. "Let's call it even, okay?"

"What do you mean, even?" He eyed me sideways.

"For last night. You falling asleep."

He huffed but said, "Fine. But if you find any more, they're mine."

I tugged at the scales of the pinecone. They scraped my fingertips, so I pulled my pocketknife out to pry off a few scales. Tiny white bugs crawled underneath, and there was another bug that looked like a miniature mealworm. Disgusting! I had to video that. Deeper in the core of the pinecone hid the tiny nuts. I shelled one, checked for bugs, and tasted it.

"Mmm . . . taste this."

"More strawberries?" He sounded hopeful, which made me feel bad that I'd eaten them all.

I handed him a pine nut and then picked a dandelion a few feet away.

Jack snorted. "Oh, you're full of surprises!"

"It's a pine nut."

"A pine what?" he asked.

"Pine. Nut. Just try it."

"Oh, good, it looks so . . . filling." Jack threw one in his mouth and scrunched his nose.

"Here. Have a dandelion too," I offered. "They taste good together."

Jack crinkled his forehead but tasted one anyway. "Not too bad, I guess. Better than I would've thought."

We stood there, munching away like rabbits with stems and leaves hanging from our mouths.

"I bet anything out here would taste good when you're this hungry," Jack said.

I agreed. The strawberries and pine nuts had flavors I'd never tasted before, like wild mountains and zesty breezes.

Just then, lightning cracked in the distance. I tensed and something caught my attention just past the cabin's outhouse. A shadow moved between the trees. It stopped and raised its head.

"Uh . . . Jack, shh!"

"What the . . . ," Jack started, but when he followed my shocked gaze over his shoulder, he froze.

The bear saw us, or smelled us, but whatever attracted her attention, she looked interested now as she raised her nose. That had to be the same bear. Had she followed us all the way to the cabin?

"Jack, let's go. Maybe she'll leave us alone."

"Like we left *her* alone last time? What if she wants revenge?"

"Don't say that." I shivered at the thought and kept one eye on the bear and the other eye on my next step toward the cabin so I wouldn't trip. "Come on, but whatever you do, don't run."

As the bear lumbered toward us, Jack stumbled, causing a few rocks to skitter downhill. The bear reared onto her hind legs—and that's when I saw her cubs, three of them, bounding through the underbrush around her. My heart thudded hard in my chest. Mother bears were known to become defensive and vicious.

"She's coming," Jack said, his voice quavering. "We have to get out of here."

But there was nowhere to hide unless we could get to the cabin before she did.

Chapter 11
Bryce

"Come on. Slowly. She's probably as afraid of us as we are of her," I whispered, remembering a story Dad told us once. He had run into a bear at a camp garbage dump and scared it away by yelling at it. He said if you act bigger than they are, they usually run. "And she's only trying to protect her cubs."

"Okay, smart aleck, whatever you say." Jack picked up a couple of rocks and cranked his arm back, ready to chuck one at the bear.

"Stop," I whispered, and we froze. "What if she attacks this time?"

She settled onto her thick legs and ambled to the

cabin, sniffing the ground. I wondered if Grandpa knew she was out there. Jack and I scrambled to hide behind a large pine tree, not that it would do us any good if she decided we were her enemy.

When the bear turned toward the river, I released my breath, hissing between my lips. "If we stay quiet, maybe she'll leave."

"I sure hope so," said Jack. "I'm starving."

Of course that's what Jack would be thinking about at a time like this.

The bears went to the river, and I turned my camera on again. Without hesitation she jumped into the water—chest deep among a group of boulders. The torrent didn't faze her at all. The cubs stood at the edge of the river, not daring to go in, bawling in distress at being separated from their mother. Jack and I crept closer for a better look.

We watched, fixated, as she pawed the water and plunged her nose into the white rapids, teasing them, daring them to overtake her. Her power matched the roaring tide as she dived in.

I was stunned when she came out of the water with a large fish wriggling in her mouth. She batted at it once, twice, lost it in the river, and, several moments later, came up with it again. After her struggle with the fish, it hung like a shining silver crescent in her mouth. She dunked it into the water and swam back to the cubs, sniffing each one as if to make sure they were hers. Soon, she ambled away, oblivious to us watching her, and disappeared into the forest with three little black bundles racing off after her.

"Wow. That was incredible," I exclaimed. "And I got it all on camera!"

Jack's eyes widened with admiration. "I wish we had *her* on our team."

I glanced sideways. "On our team? What do you mean?"

"I mean, look at her fish. I want that fish." Envy thickened his voice. "Maybe we could go fishing down there, too."

"Maybe." I thought for a moment. "It's really steep though. Not a place we could get in to go fishing. Not like her." My stomach growled out loud, but I didn't care. I was going to be famous on YouTube.

We hurried to the cabin where Jack beelined it to the pantry and opened a can of beans. Grandpa wasn't in the main room, and the bedroom door was shut. I could hear him snoring like a bear, though. He'd be bummed that he'd missed the show. At least he could watch my video.

Jack and I took turns digging our forks into the beans, not caring about who had germs. Jack took two bites in a row. I grabbed the can. "Save some for me!"

"I am," he said, even though I knew he wouldn't if I didn't stand up for myself.

We were both hungry. I'd have to check the traps soon, but I was afraid to go outside knowing the bear was nearby.

Chapter 12
Bryce

When Grandpa woke up, I showed him my video of the bear.

"I've never seen anything like that in person," he said, shaking his head. "At least you caught it on video. That one's a keeper."

My chest swelled with pride. I wished Grandpa could have been with us too, but at least he was proud of me.

Grandpa continued, "But, guys, seriously, we need to be even more careful now that we know she's got cubs she's protecting. We don't want her to think we mean any harm. Or that we have food for her. Did you see which way they went?"

I shook my head. "They could be close, but they went downhill."

"Let's just stay together when we go out," said Grandpa. "I don't think she's a danger to us as long as we stay calm, but still, we don't want to be caught by surprise, nose-to-nose, with her out there."

The three of us looked out the door for a minute, scanning the forest. When all was clear, we sneaked to the stream to check on the traps.

On the way, I showed Jack how to walk quietly on the spongy, pine-needle ground. For a moment he followed my advice, stepping carefully over the crackling, knobby twigs. I don't know why, but he suddenly stomped off like a bumbling giant, louder than a herd of deer.

"Cut it out, Jack," I hissed, and Grandpa snorted. "You'll scare off our dinner."

Jack exaggerated his tiptoeing, taking high-kneed steps. He was so frustrating sometimes.

"Stop being so worried about everything," Jack scoffed.

Didn't he care that the bear might be startled by his brash movements? It seemed like he didn't realize his actions could cause problems for all of us. Why didn't he ever stop to think first?

Grandpa turned toward the river. "Quiet down, Jack," he said. "I'll go look for the bear."

"Okay." I didn't want him to leave us, but I wondered if he was hoping to catch the bear in action too. Grandpa was known to do daring things, especially when he was younger, like stand outside in severe thunderstorms hoping to see a tornado. *Thrill-seeker*, I'd heard Mom say when they were deciding if they should let us go on the trip with Grandpa. It's why Dad was supposed to come along too. He was definitely more cautious than Grandpa.

But I trusted Grandpa. He'd never do anything to put us in danger.

Close to one of the traps, Jack and I crouched behind a group of scrubby bushes. But its noose hung limp and empty. My heart dropped into my growling stomach. I wanted a thick, juicy cheeseburger with a fresh tomato and lettuce from Mom's garden. My eyes watered as I daydreamed about food, or maybe the tears were from missing Mom. She had barely let me go backpacking as it was, once Dad cancelled. I begged her and promised a million times I wouldn't get into any trouble.

"So, now what do we do, genius?" asked Jack.

"There's one more trap up the mountain," I said, hoping I wasn't a total failure in the survival department.

"Shh . . . look." Jack pointed toward the stream.

I spotted it right away. Some kind of a duck waddling away from us.

Jack stooped down and duck-walked after it, looking ridiculous. I was angry that he followed it because, sure enough, the duck flew away and landed on the other side of the river.

I growled, thinking about how the bear would probably have a gourmet supper of duck and trout tonight while we snacked on random, mismatched food.

"Stupid bird!" Jack yelled after it and laughed as if he'd heard the funniest joke.

"What were you thinking?" I ran my hands through my hair. "We could have had it for dinner."

"I thought I could catch it."

"With what? Your bare hands?" I asked.

"Did you have a better idea?"

"I don't know. I needed a minute to think about it. Sometimes you have to stop and think about things!" I trudged uphill to the last trap. Jack trailed behind me, but I wasn't going to give him the time of day.

"Gah! We'll find something else to eat."

I ignored him. Why was it that he complained about having to babysit *me*? He was the one causing all the problems out here.

As I closed in on the third trap, I raised my hand, signaling Jack to stop. Like a bandit spying out the enemy, I squatted behind a group of boulders. A golden-brown furry lump about the size of a small soccer ball lay in the trap.

I picked my way along the rocks toward the dead animal.

"What is it?" asked Jack.

I nudged it with my hiking boot, making sure it was dead. It reminded me of a fat groundhog. "A marmot, I think." I untangled it from the noose and sticks. "Maybe it'll taste like duck if we're lucky."

"Are you sure we can eat it?"

"It's meat, isn't it? And we don't have much of a choice now, do we?" I picked up the marmot and shoved it at Jack.

He yelped and jumped back. "Stop it!"

"What? Afraid of a little furry animal?" I teased. Jack hated hunting and got all squeamish around blood. I knew it was a low blow, but I was so annoyed at him. That duck would've tasted way better, but at least we had fresh meat.

I carried it to the porch where Grandpa waited for us.

"Did you see the bear?" I asked.

"Nope. No sign of her," he said, "or the cubs. What did you catch?"

I held it up and asked, "A marmot?"

He nodded. "Yep. It's a big one. That must have been some trap you set."

I smiled, glad to make him proud again. I wondered if there was a way to compile all the good things I'd done to offset the sure disappointment he'd have in me when he found out I was lying to him. I gulped. "Um . . . where should I skin it?"

"I'll get a cutting board. Take it close to the stream. I'll start the fire inside."

At the stream I cut into the marmot under its front shoulder and stuck my finger in, unsure at first. I struggled to pull the skin off the body and down the back legs. It was much thicker and tougher than skinning a rabbit. A mess of blood and guts covered my hands.

"Jack! I need your help!"

He jogged over. "What?"

"Put your hand under the skin here and pull on it. I'll pull on this side."

"No way. I'm not touching that." His face scrunched into a scowl, and he turned his head away.

"I need your help. You can wash your hands when you're done." I rubbed my nose with my arm, trying to avoid the smell of raw meat, blood, and dirty fur.

He shook his head and turned away.

"Come on, wimp!"

That got his attention. He grimaced again and stifled a gag. He held the marmot away from his body as I pulled the skin off. Once we stripped off most of the skin, I sawed the head off and broke the legs. Next, I sliced open its chest and belly to gut it. The stench was even stronger. It even made my stomach roll. That's when Jack walked away.

"Seriously?"

"Dude, I'm gonna lose it." He bent over and heaved. Not much came out. He leaned over for another moment before wiping his mouth with his sleeve. He glanced at the marmot and shivered.

Jack was such a sissy. And, again, I wondered why he always treated *me* like the baby? I bent my head over the meat and cut deeper into the body. I was probably expending more calories preparing our meal than I'd get from eating it, no thanks to Jack.

Angry, I cut harder. *Scrape. Scrape. Thwack.* I hit a bone.

Jack's hiking boots appeared in front of me, but I refused to look up at him. It made me dig harder into the marmot. My knife twisted in my hand, slipped, and ripped the skin off my thumb. My blood poured out and mixed with the marmot's blood. I yelped and jumped up from my crouched position.

"Put pressure on it," Jack insisted as he almost threw up again.

He turned and stumbled away to the cabin.

"Where are you going?" The pain fueled my anger. He was the most selfish and cowardly person I'd ever known.

I covered my thumb with my T-shirt and squeezed it to stop the bleeding. My head swirled, and a tunnel of stars closed in on my vision. The last thing I needed was to pass out. I sat on a log and lowered my head between my legs. I couldn't believe Jack left at the first sight of my blood. I breathed deeply and held my hand above my head.

A few minutes later, Grandpa showed up with Jack, holding a water bottle and the first aid kit. Jack poured water on my cut and tore open a large bandage.

It surprised me to see Jack actually helping. I didn't want to admit it, but I'd misjudged him. I wasn't used to him being kind to me.

"You all right?" asked Grandpa.

I nodded, embarrassed at how I'd let my anger go and made another stupid mistake.

"Boys, listen." Grandpa sat beside me on the log. "We're out here to have a good time, but you both need to be more careful and work together. There's no sense in being at odds with each other, believe me. Someday, you'll only have each other to rely on. Your parents will be gone. I'll be gone."

He tipped his head to the side. "Even most of your friends you have now might be gone. And then what? Who will you go to then? You'll always be able to count on each other, so you need to work at your relationship now. Put each other first. Learn how to be friends. Learn how to be brothers."

Jack hung his head, nodding. He stooped to pick up the bandages that had spilled to the ground. "You okay?" he asked me.

"Yeah." I breathed deeply through my nose to clear the pain. I felt oddly grateful to him. "Thanks."

Jack nodded. "I'm gonna go wash up and fill the water bottle."

"Grandpa," I started, building up the nerve to tell him about the pictures and the map. "I need to tell you—"

"I know." Grandpa cut me off. "You and Jack just don't see eye to eye all the time, but that's okay. You're two very different people, but, I promise you, those differences will come in handy when you least expect it."

I sighed. Keeping a secret from him was eating away at me, but he seemed really concerned about me and Jack, so I let the map go for now.

A few minutes later, I told Grandpa, "I don't think I can finish gutting the marmot." My hand was throbbing. I'd already soaked through the bandage and struggled to replace it with a clean one.

"I'll do it," Jack said, arriving back from the cabin with the water filter.

While Grandpa wrapped my hand in gauze, Jack positioned himself over the marmot. Even though he held the knife awkwardly and gagged twice, he managed to clean out the guts, following my instructions.

Maybe there was still hope for us. We were brothers, after all.

Chapter 13
Jack

That night I agreed to play UNO with Bryce but only to stop him from annoying me by sticking his camera in my face and his adventure jabber. He acted like he was the king of the mountain and knew it all out there. I could figure these things out too, if I wanted to.

While we played, Grandpa rubbed spices on the meat. "Did you guys see any bigger logs out there?" he asked.

Bryce and I answered at the same time. "Nope." I don't think either of us wanted to go back out there in the dark.

"Who wants to go find some?" Grandpa set the cast-iron pan on the grate in the fireplace.

With raised eyebrows, Bryce sighed and shot a glance toward the door. He smirked and tilted his head as if he was testing me. "Your turn this time, and while you're at it, check the traps." He laid down a "Draw Two" card.

I clenched my jaw and glared at him, not wanting to argue in front of Grandpa after the talk he'd had with us earlier about getting along. I made an effort to be nice. "Let's go together."

"I'll keep watch from the porch," Grandpa offered.

Trying to freak Bryce out, I whispered, "What if the bear's out there hunting and eating off the traps, waiting for us to come out?"

"Jeez! Don't say that!" Bryce shivered.

I opened the door and watched the firelight spread its warm glow a few feet into the darkness. I stood there for a moment, listening to the night sounds and letting my eyes adjust.

A branch snapped to my right, followed by a scurrying sound disappearing toward the river. The shadows of the trees in between the dappled moonlight hid whatever was creeping around.

"Probably just a small animal," Bryce said, sounding overly confident as usual.

"Why do you say that?" I asked.

"A bear wouldn't make a fast scurrying sound like that. It's probably a raccoon."

Even though he was such a know-it-all, he wasn't the first one to take a step off the porch. I was, but as I did, something flapped near our heads, and Bryce stifled a yelp.

Grandpa poked his head out. "What is it?"

"A bat, I think." I shrugged, trying to make light of it.

I brushed my hand through my hair. "Let's go." I picked up a rock, just in case I needed to defend myself.

Bryce picked one up, too. He always had to copy me. But then he threw it into the trees.

"In case there's an animal out there waiting for us," he said.

Not a bad idea, I thought. I held the flashlight up, unsure about using it. What if it allowed an animal to see us better? I didn't want to be under a spotlight, so I hunkered down, shielding the light with my hand. Crazy shadows danced around us, making it impossible to see what might be out there. It felt like hidden eyes were following us, waiting to attack.

"There's a long branch. I think it's thick enough." My voice pierced the darkness with a fearful high pitch. I needed to calm down. If animals could smell fear, no doubt they could hear it too. "Help me drag it to the porch."

"Find one?" Grandpa asked, standing in the glowing doorway.

Bryce grabbed a branch, and I took the trunk. I was pretty sure I was doing all the lifting. When we got to the porch, I finally relaxed. Grandpa handed me the axe and gave Bryce a small saw. We worked at cutting the branch into small pieces for the fire.

The rest of the night consisted of one chore after the other. Chopping wood, adding it to the fire, helping Grandpa cook, washing dishes, dusting and sweeping the cabin. I kept wondering when I'd get some downtime to hang out and check my phone. Sophie probably thought I hated her by now.

"When'll the meat be ready?" I asked Grandpa.

"Soon. I want to make sure it's really well-done so we don't get sick from it."

I finally pulled out my phone and realized it was almost out of battery. "I thought I turned it off," I whispered to myself. How could that be? I turned it around in my hand, looking it over as if it would magically answer me.

I heard a chuckle and turned to see Bryce laughing with his hand clapped over his mouth.

I pointed at him. "Did you . . . ?"

"I didn't touch it. I swear!"

How could it have died so fast? Now what was I going to do?

Grandpa announced that the meat was done and set it aside to cool. He sawed off a chunk for each of us, set it on our plates, and said grace. It took me at least a minute to cut a piece off and even longer to chew it. It was one of the worst things I'd ever eaten—tough, leathery, and burnt on the outside. None of the spices tasted like they had made it through the inferno. I chewed for a long time without actually swallowing. My jaw hurt, and I spit the meat into my napkin. I went to the pantry and opted for a few spoonfuls of peanut butter instead. Plus, I was tired enough to call it a night.

After some water to wash it all down, I pulled out my sleeping bag, flipped off my shoes, and found a spot on the floor. I didn't have the energy to fight Bryce for the couch.

As I crawled into my sleeping bag, he complained that I was getting out of cleaning up supper. I covered my head, checked for reception, which I didn't have at all, and played a game on my phone until it completely ran out of battery.

Soon the fire was out. Everything was quiet aside from

the roaring river outside, which reminded me of Mom. She loved camping beside rivers because of the soothing, rushing sound. I didn't know why she couldn't have been with us. Maybe if she would have come, Dad would have too. But neither of them had been to Colorado in a long time. Either they didn't like Grandpa, or they wanted to get rid of me and Bryce for part of the summer. Well, me at least, since Bryce was her golden child. I knew she didn't want to get rid of him.

I bit back my resentment, remembering the night before when I thought I was going to die by bear attack. I had to find a way to make things better between Mom and me. I just couldn't figure out how.

And no matter what I did, I kept messing up.

Chapter 14
Bryce

Sunshine radiated through the window. In a fog-like state between sleep and wakefulness, I dreamed of a lazy morning at home. A Saturday morning filled with pancakes, and bacon, and . . .

I fought to stay in the moment, but a gut-wrenching pain pulled me up out of sleep like a marionette on strings. I doubled over, realizing I needed to find a toilet of some kind, and quick.

Shivering, I reached for my jacket and hobbled to the door, where my gray hiking boots sat. I didn't even have time to put them on. I threw open the door and bounded down the steps in the direction of the outhouse, about fifty feet from the cabin. When I was ten feet away, I couldn't wait one more second. I had to pull down my pants and squat by a tree. Never before had I experienced such pain wracking my insides. I groaned loudly sure I was going to die there in my own waste.

A few minutes later, another episode of panting and sweating hit me. I heaved and threw up. It must have been the marmot. The thought of it made me sick again.

When I was finally empty, I plucked off leaves from a nearby bush to wipe myself. As I stood to pull up my boxers and jeans, a head rush forced me to lean into a tree for balance. After a few deep breaths, I shuffled back to the cabin. Jack was standing in the doorway, scowling.

"Dude, did you just puke?" He backed up as I stumbled inside.

I grunted and collapsed onto the couch, curling into a ball.

"What happened?"

I grunted again. I wanted him to disappear and leave me alone to die.

"I'll get you some water to flush out whatever's bugging you."

"Whatever's bugging me?" I groaned. "You're bugging me." I rolled over and hoped Jack had left me in my misery.

Twice more that morning, the pain ravaged through me. Grandpa kept making me drink water. He wasn't feeling so great, either. All I wanted to do was go home. Enough of this survival crap. Mom would know how to make it better.

By noon, after a few more trips to the forest and a long nap, I must have been ten pounds lighter. But at least I could stand up without any pain.

"Good morning, sunshine!" Jack repeated Dad's annoying, early-morning line with thick sarcasm. "Feel better?"

"Yeah, I think so." I winced at another mild cramp.

"I hate to remind you now, but want to go fishing at the lake?" Jack shut the book he was reading. "I've been waiting all morning for you to get it together."

"Go ahead. You don't need me."

With a cocked eyebrow, he said, "Yeah, right, like I'm gonna go out there alone with that bear wandering around."

I sat down at the kitchen table and rubbed my forehead.

"Here, look at this." Jack lifted the book.

"What is it?" I noticed it was a journal. "Whose is it?" I hesitated to open it, sure we shouldn't be sneaking through someone's journal—probably Grandpa's. I'd already done enough sneaking in his stuff to last me for a long time.

"It's Grandpa's. Grandma wrote in it too. He said we could read it." Jack opened the faded purple cover.

I noticed my hand was shaky when I reached for it. Grandpa's telltale boxy handwriting read:

. . . I never sleep as soundly as I do here. I took Eliana to the lake for the first time yesterday. She can't believe we're so lucky to have this place all to ourselves. I can't either. We caught two large trout for dinner. She wants to go again tomorrow, despite the climb . . .

"So about those fish?" The lake in Grandpa's journal had to be the same lake on the map—Lure Lake. It was pulling at me, almost daring me to find it. No matter how sick I felt, we had to go. I couldn't wait any longer.

"Think you can make it to the lake?" Jack reached for the journal as Grandpa came in from outside. "It shouldn't be too far up the river from what I remember, right, Grandpa?"

"The lake? Yeah, it's about a two-hour hike," Grandpa said.

"Sure, I'll go." I nodded, determined. "If the hike doesn't kill me, the hunger will, so I'll give it a try."

"Are you coming too?" Jack asked Grandpa.

He groaned a bit and rubbed his stomach. "I'll let you two go up today. I've had to make about five runs to the outhouse this morning. But promise me you'll stay together and take it easy. No showing off. And if you run into the bear, just come on back."

"I'm not in any kind of mood to show off," I said, rubbing my hollow stomach.

Wide-eyed, Jack shook his head. "Me neither."

I looked at Jack, hoping he really meant it.

"I'm trusting you, Jack, to take care of your brother." Grandpa handed a walkie-talkie to him. "Call me if you need anything, and call me when you get there." They made sure the dials were on the same channel and tested them.

"Got it." Jack nodded and stuffed his backpack with the first aid kit, walkie-talkie, fishing supplies and pole, our knives, ponchos, water, and some snacks.

"Take the rope too," Grandpa said.

I tossed the rope to Jack. He tied it to the outside of the backpack. I grabbed my video camera, sneaked the map into my pocket, and pulled on my boots.

"Maybe you should eat a power bar so you have energy for the hike," Jack suggested.

"Ugh. Don't even mention food. But go ahead, you can have yours."

Jack had already unwrapped his power bar and was stuffing it in his mouth.

My aching body barely made it out the door after Jack. At least I didn't have to lug a backpack. "Bye, Grandpa." I waved and, before I knew it, patted my pocket where the map was—a subconscious move dictated by my guilt.

"I'll be expecting you back by six, seven at the latest. Well before dusk, okay?"

"Okay. Hope you feel better soon." I noticed he looked kind of pale.

"You too. Take it easy." He smiled and gave me a wink.

I wish I felt as carefree and could wink back. But between my shrunken gut and the guilt swirling in me, I could barely manage a smile.

Chapter 15
Bryce

At the stream, I splashed water in my face and rinsed out my mouth. A cool breeze jarred me awake as we crossed the stream on two wobbly rocks leading us up the trail.

I'd been in a haze all morning but finally shook it off as we picked our way alongside the cascading river. Even though I was still tired, hope and purpose surged in me knowing we'd have good food soon, and I'd hopefully find the treasure.

I debated again whether I should tell Jack about it or not. He might just make fun of me for being worried. I decided to wait until I knew what I was looking for.

Maybe it wouldn't even be a big deal, not something Jack would care about. Maybe there was a stash of gold hidden or a bunch of long-forgotten jewels. The more I daydreamed about it, the more it puzzled me. Why would the map be in the box along with the pictures of my parents? Maybe the treasure had to do with them. What if it was something they'd hidden there? But if that was the case, why wouldn't they have ever wanted to come back to recover what had been hidden? Or maybe the last time we were all here, they'd already gotten it and the map had been long forgotten. The more I thought about it, the more all the possibilities tangled together in a cloudy web. It didn't make sense.

The canyon narrowed as we hiked, forming a steep gorge. Remembering the topo maps, I knew the only other way to the lake was to go miles up and around the mountains because the river created such a steep gorge. I turned my camera to the white frothy rapids and waterfalls tumbling into each other. We were forced to start climbing along the rock walls because the flooded river had washed out the trail. We didn't have any other choice but to climb.

Jack stopped and eyed the path we would have to take. "Do you think we should turn back?"

"Uh . . ." I wasn't sure what to say. I really wanted to keep going. "It doesn't look too hard."

"Okay." Jack moved effortlessly along the cliff, his long arms and legs able to reach much farther than mine.

My legs felt like rubber before we'd even started. I'd have to take it slow.

Dad had taken us on harder routes before, but always with safety gear. Now we only had Grandpa's old rope. No harness to hang from. No grippy, rock-climbing shoes.

No chalk to keep our hands from slipping or helmets to protect our heads. It made me nervous, but I kept on climbing after Jack.

Soon, instead of wide ridges and outcroppings to scramble on, small cracks and pockets in the rock were all I could find.

Jack hooked his arm over a small ledge in the rock and peered at me. "You okay?"

I nodded and freed one hand to push strands of my dark, greasy hair out of my eyes.

"Come on, then," he said, creasing his brow and sounding annoyed. "If you take so long, we'll both run out of energy."

I breathed deeply. "Go ahead. I'm fine." Jack could climb a lot faster than me. I just needed to take my time. Not make a wrong move.

Jack nodded and kept going. I shook out one hand and then the other, taking a break on a narrow ledge. I took another deep breath and continued on, hand over hand, telling myself not to look down and that I would make it.

You have to, the map seemed to whisper to me. *You have to uncover the treasure.*

Chapter 16

Jack

The climb took way longer than it should have because of Bryce, but we finally made it. Lure Lake spread out ahead of us like a blue mirror at the base of three mountain peaks. Puffy white clouds hung above them in the sky.

I turned to make sure Bryce got to the top of the last cliff. "There it is." I pointed.

He grimaced, pulling himself up. Catching his first glimpse of the lake, he smiled. "Wow."

"Yeah, wow." I most definitely agreed and handed Bryce my canteen. We walked along the mossy rock path to the west side of the lake. I found a spot along the bank that wasn't too muddy and set my backpack down. "This look good?" I took out the tackle box, looking for a good lure. I wished we had two poles. Bryce was probably going to hog it. Trying my best to be the good brother that Grandpa wanted me to be, I handed it to him. "Want to fish first?"

"Uh . . . sure?" He sounded skeptical, like I was going to trick him.

I let him dig through the tackle box. He settled on a rooster tail spinner, tied it on, and walked to the edge of the water. I called Grandpa on the walkie-talkie to let him know we'd made it safe and sound.

"This might take a while," Bryce said. "I don't see much movement out there yet."

"It's okay. Not like we've got anywhere to go." I squatted down to feel the water. Ice cold. It'd feel great on my sweaty feet. I yanked off my shoes and socks and waded in up to my shins. I could tell it got a lot deeper after that.

Ten minutes later, Bryce had only gotten a couple of nibbles.

"Let me try for a bit," I suggested.

He shrugged and handed me the pole. "I'm gonna go explore around the lake a bit."

"I don't know . . ." I looked across the lake. It wasn't that far. "Just stay where I can see you." I didn't want anything else to happen to the golden prince, especially not on my watch. Mom and Dad and Grandpa would kill me.

Bryce walked north toward the peaks and rounded the lake. Even though it made me nervous, I figured, even if he encountered a bear, he could make his way back in just a few minutes.

"Bryce!" I shouted across the lake to check how easy it was to hear each other.

He turned, waved, and yelled, "What?"

Not bad. "Just checking!" I didn't want anything to happen. Didn't want to let Grandpa down again.

I cast my line out, found a rock to sit on, and slumped forward. I slowly reeled it in. Fishing wasn't my favorite, but I did love Grandpa's fresh-cooked trout. Plus, I felt like I'd been close to starving since we'd been on our trip.

I watched the clear water and could've sworn there were shadows of fish darting around. Why weren't they biting? I poked around in the tackle box for a different lure and picked one that looked like a green fly that Bryce had made at some fly-fishing class he took. He did stuff like that. And I played football.

I glanced up and saw him across the lake. He was bent over, looking at the ground. He stood, walked a few feet more, and looked behind a tree stump.

"What're you doing?" I shouted.

He looked up, pointed downward, and yelled, "Nothing. Just some cool rocks."

He was such a nerd. Why did he care so much about dumb rocks? He even had a collection at home. When he was little he tried to sell them in our neighborhood. No one but Mom ever bought any.

Distracted with daydreaming, I nearly missed the fishing line bobbing, once, twice. I jerked the pole up. The line bobbed again, and I felt the strain of the line. "I got one!" I reeled it in without much of a fight. It was only a ten-incher, but it was something. A few more and we'd be able to head back soon.

When I looked up again, I couldn't see Bryce anymore.

Where had he gone? There wasn't much he could be hiding behind, just a few boulders, scattered trees, and bushes. "Bryce! Where are you?" I called, still clinging to the flopping fish. "Bryce!" I shouted even louder, feeling panic rise in my chest.

I set the fish down on the rocks and started to walk along the path. How could I have lost track of him so quickly? I looked again and still couldn't see him. I started to run, jumping from one rock to the next. "Bryce!"

"I'm right here." He appeared from behind a pine tree and waved.

My panic sputtered out of me, turning into anger. I yelled, "Don't disappear again!"

"Okay! Sorry! I'll be back in a minute!"

"What did you find?"

"Nothing. Just some animal tracks I'm trying to figure out!"

Relieved, but still mad, I went back to the fish, unhooked it, and started fishing again so we could leave soon.

I looked up at Bryce again. He sure was acting strange, like he was up to something. And I was starting to get a bad feeling. I looked around to make sure the bear was nowhere in sight. Maybe I was anxious because Bryce scared me. I needed to calm down. Everything was going to be fine. I just wanted to get back to the cabin as soon as possible before anything else could happen.

Chapter 17

Bryce

Getting away from Jack was the easy part. My heart was pounding, nervous that Jack would see through me and know I was hiding something from him.

On the other side of the lake were several trees and a burnt tree trunk that looked like it had gotten struck by lightning. It could take all day to dig around each tree and find the treasure. What was I thinking?

I wove my way through the trees. Looking for . . . what? I didn't know. Looking for something out of the ordinary. An X, like on the map. Or maybe a special rock. Some kind of treasure. Whatever it was, I hoped it was still there and that I'd know it when I found it.

I stopped in my tracks to clear my mind and thought back to some of my favorite books and movies that had treasures in them. Often there wasn't anything out of the ordinary marking a treasure or a secret. It wasn't meant to be found. It was meant to stay hidden. If it was Grandpa's secret, probably only he knew where it was, or maybe my parents.

Jack kept yelling and distracting me from my search. I hoped it would take him a long time to catch a few fish. I didn't want him coming over and messing things up for me.

I worked my way from tree to tree, scouting the ground around them. I kicked over rocks and pulled back clumps of moss and pine needles, but I didn't find anything obvious. What if those men we met on the path really had gotten here first?

It made me angry that they might've taken something that wasn't theirs. But who was I kidding? I pulled the map out of my pocket, which *I'd* taken from Grandpa, and looked at it again. Had I missed something?

I checked the angle of the river to the lake and where the tree was on the map. If the map was accurate, I needed to walk a bit farther south, farther away from Jack.

"Got another one!" he yelled again.

I waved and yelled, "Great! Keep it up!"

"Come on back," he shouted.

"In a minute." I walked from one tree to the other, nervous I'd run out of time and not find a thing.

Finally, I saw something odd on a tree trunk, facing away from the lake. I squatted down and looked at the bark of the pine tree. It had been carved into. I ran my fingers over the scarred letters.

Will Harrison

2002

Could that be it? The treasure?

"Come on," Jack yelled, more impatiently.

Who could Will Harrison be? I mean, Harrison was our last name. But who was Will? A cousin? A long-lost uncle? And 2002? Is that when this Will was here? Or—I swallowed hard—did he die then? 2002 was before I was born, so I would have no idea who Will was. I dug around the tree, looking for something else that might be buried there.

"Come on! Grandpa's going to be mad!" Jack was waving me back.

"Okay! Hang on!" I needed time to think. Had someone died and was buried up here? That was creepy. Was that even legal?

I looked around for something else, like a box or a special rock or a grave marker. I'd have to ask Grandpa about our relatives sometime. Ask in a casual way so he wouldn't suspect anything.

Part of me was disappointed at what I'd found. Not a cool treasure or a long-lost secret hiding place. There had to be something else here.

"Bryce! I mean it. If you don't come back now, I'm going to call Grandpa."

"Hang on! I found something cool."

Jack bent to pack the fishing gear. I figured I had about two more minutes before he'd get mad enough to come get me. Trying to avoid using my sore thumb, I dug into the rocky soil around the base of the tree, desperate to find something to qualify as a treasure. My finger nails scraped on something hard and smooth. I banged on it and could tell it was metal. My heart hammered in my chest. I found it!

I used a pointed rock to dig and pry out a metal box. It was about the size of a small shoebox, like one of Grandma's old rectangle-shaped cookie tins I'd seen in the hayloft. My fingers were rubbed raw from digging, but I had no time to lose. I wiped the dirt off the top of it and wiggled it open.

My heart raced as I lifted a familiar-looking, small wooden box out of the metal tin. The box was kind of like the one I'd found in the file folder, but more similar to the boxes Grandpa had carved for me and Jack when we were babies. I used mine at home to put cool rocks in. Jack kept his on his desk with his coin collection in it.

I turned the box in my hand and opened it. There were a bunch of dried flower petals laying around a small satchel and an old-looking gold coin like one in Jack's collection. I wondered how much it might be worth, but I wasn't tempted to take it. I already had theft on my guilty conscious. I didn't need to add to it.

As I picked up the satchel to look inside, Jack interrupted my search. "Bryce! Let's go! Now!"

He had the walkie-talkie in hand. That was it. I had to go.

I waved at him and yelled, "Okay!" I peeked inside the little bag and thought I saw some kind of a band or bracelet but thought better of taking more time. Maybe we'd get another chance to come back. I could dig around more, now that I knew where it was. I put everything back and reburied the metal box so it wouldn't be obvious to someone passing by.

"Coming!" I yelled. I ran my fingers over the letters of Will's name on the tree before I waved to Jack again. I jogged around the lake to meet him, leaving with more questions than I'd brought with me.

Chapter 18
Bryce

What were you doing over there?" asked Jack.

"Pfft. Nothing. Just looking for something cool to add to my collection." It wasn't a complete lie. I did have a nature collection at home, sitting on my windowsill, but Grandpa's treasure was not going to join it.

Jack shook his head and sighed. "Let's go. I don't want Grandpa to worry."

We walked around the lake toward the cliffs. I picked dirt from my fingernails and adjusted the bandage on my hand. The sun was behind the mountains, but it would be a long time before it got dark. I followed in Jack's footsteps and asked, "How many fish did you catch?"

He didn't answer for a moment, probably still mad at me. "Three small ones, but they'll do for supper."

Good, I thought, *that means we'll have to come back again to get more fish.* It would give me time to finish looking through the box.

"What were you doing over there?"

"Just looking around . . . you know."

Jack shook his head and glanced back at me. "No, I don't know. You scared me. I thought the bear got you or something."

Before we started climbing back down, Jack called Grandpa on the walkie-talkie to tell him we were heading back. It sounded pretty crackly, but we could understand Grandpa's voice well enough. "I'm feeling better. Can't wait to eat some trout. Take your time coming down."

We started our climb into the canyon in silence. After a few minutes, I blurted out, above the roar of the river, "Jack! Do you know if we have a relative named Will?" That came out sounding way too random. I'd have to be more subtle with him or he'd wonder what I was up to.

His eyebrows pinched together, and he looked at me sideways. "No. Why?"

"Oh, I dunno. Just heard Grandpa mention him the other day." Another lie. "But I didn't know who he was." I didn't like how many lies I was accumulating to cover up my search.

"Okaaay." Jack probably thought I was losing it, but I didn't care as long as he didn't suspect anything. After this trip, I'd sneak the map and photos to the hayloft like nothing had ever happened. No one needed to know what I'd found. But the questions were starting to tug at me even more than before.

I stumbled after Jack along an old rockslide and shouted, "Do you know if a relative of ours died in 2002?"

"How would I know? I was a baby," Jack yelled over his shoulder. "What's up with all the random questions?" He shimmied around a rock outcropping.

I tried not to think about how close we were to the river's edge. The water roiled and churned down the canyon.

I shrugged. "Just curious."

"Okay, well, keep 'em to yourself and focus on your step." He reached toward a clear line of handholds on the cliff. But it was higher than I wanted to go. I couldn't see another way without getting too close to the river, so I followed him.

I wiped loose rock off a small ridge so I wouldn't slip. Even when I was at my best, it was challenging to keep up with Jack. He was bigger, stronger, and more athletic than me by a mile.

My rubbery legs shuddered as I scrambled to find a sturdy spot to stand on. I couldn't believe I already needed a break. We'd only just started. Maybe I should have eaten a power bar first. I hadn't eaten anything all day.

"Jack! Wait up." I watched as he climbed effortlessly about ten feet ahead of me. I was maybe ten feet or so above the river even though it felt more like fifty. The angle wasn't totally vertical, so even if we slipped, I should be able to catch myself.

"I am," Jack shouted and looked back. "Are you okay?"

I raised my eyebrows, too tired to shout, and whispered to myself, "My hand's killing me." The bandage was ripped and frayed, and my fingertips felt raw from digging the box out of the ground. I squeezed my eyes, trying to ignore the pain.

"You can rest over here." Jack coaxed me to a ledge where he was standing. Near him, some rocks fell. I followed them with my eyes, staring at where they avalanched into the river. Looking down was a mistake. The swirls in the water rushing past us were dizzying. I gasped for air as if I was already drowning.

But it wasn't air that I needed.

I needed hard, solid ground to stand on.

Jack gaped at me with frantic, wide eyes.

My breathing quickened. I clung to the wall with all my strength, willing myself to become glued to the rock. Every ounce of my body and my mind focused in on one thing—survival.

"Come on, Bryce! Get it together," Jack demanded. "Just a few more feet. You can do it."

I sucked in a shaky breath, looking up and around for a way out. The route Jack had taken with his long arms was out of reach. The cold rock cut into my sweaty hands. My big, clumsy hiking boots didn't fit into the smaller footholds nearby.

"Move your left foot a step higher to that hole," Jack commanded. "Then move your right foot over a bit."

"I can't. I'm stuck!" My words squeezed out an octave higher than normal. Short, quick breaths overtook my lungs. My foot felt like it was going to slip.

"Bryce. Listen to me!" he barked sharply, sounding like Dad. "You can do this! Stop panicking. Take a deep breath, and do what I tell you." His eyes zeroed in on me. I could see a sheen of sweat on his forehead.

I drew in a chestful of air, but as I did, my good hand

slid a fraction of an inch. A shot of adrenaline coursed through me. My hiking boot fumbled at the last inch of space on the crumbling foothold.

And then, I was falling.

A scream burst through the air.

A dull thud filled my ears.

All was dark.

And I was gone.

Chapter 19
Jack

I begged Bryce to stop looking down and keep moving, but he panicked and froze. All I heard over the roar of the menacing river was the hiss of his quick, short breaths. All I could think of was how Grandpa told me to watch out for him and not let anything happen.

I had unclipped the climbing rope from the backpack, but I couldn't figure out how to use it to help Bryce. It hung over my arm, limp and useless. As useless as my brain.

All he needed to do was reach a foot farther to a clean handhold, but it might as well have been a mile long because, clearly, he was too short. He'd have to find another way. Honestly, I couldn't see another way from where I was, but still, I tried to help him. I really did.

His right foot shook and slipped. His right hand grappled at the handhold. There was little hope for him to recover the imbalance in his weight. I could see the helpless, questioning look in his bluish-gray eyes. I backtracked a few steps, but I wasn't quick enough.

As if in slow motion, he swung like a barn door, twisting away from the cliff. My heart wrenched and tore away, falling with him. I reached out as he fell ten or fifteen feet and hit the canyon floor.

Stunned, my heart felt like it stopped. I couldn't breathe. Seconds passed. Minutes?

When I exhaled, a deep, moaning "Bryce!" came out of me.

I trembled at a sickening rise in my stomach. I hoped he was simply shocked, would soon open his eyes and move. But he lay there motionless, contorted on his back, and tangled in a scraggly bush on a small, dry ledge, only a few feet from the river.

When my voice finally worked, I yelled over and over again, "Bryce! Are you okay?"

No response. No movement. Nothing.

"Bryce! Get up! Come on!"

I clambered down the cliff so fast I nearly fell. When I reached him, I knelt over him, yelling and willing him awake, but he still didn't move. I looked around frantically. My eyes darted, searching for an answer to what I'd just seen. It couldn't be real.

I put my ear to Bryce's chest. I couldn't tell if he was breathing—there was so much noise. Noise from the river. Noise from my sobbing. I needed to calm down and breathe.

What had just happened? Could it be a dream? I wanted to spin the clock back thirty minutes and restart the climb. I could do that, couldn't I?

I laid my ear against his mouth to feel for air coming out. Nothing. I ran my fingers under his chin to check for a pulse. Still, nothing. Maybe I wasn't checking the right place. I searched his neck, urging a ripple to start, anything to signal he was alive. But I couldn't find it.

My hands moved too fast from his neck to his chest to his wrist and back again. I closed my eyes, took a deep breath, and lifted Bryce's wrist from the bush. I felt again for a pulse. Moments passed. I could only feel my own pounding heartbeat, too strong and fast to be his.

I sat there, shaking my head in my hands, disbelieving my brother was really gone. He'd wake up. He had to. I felt alongside his neck again and took my time.

After a long moment, I thought I found it, but I wasn't sure. It was too slow to be my heartbeat: a slow, faint pulse. I didn't move again for a minute, making sure my imagination wasn't playing tricks on me.

Thump, thump. Thump, thump. There it was again. Faint and drawn-out, but it was really there!

He was alive?

Oh my gosh, he's alive, I thought. *Now what do I do?*

I bent over him again, wanting to hug him, wanting him to wake up.

I shook his shoulder gently and yelled, "Bryce! Wake up!" I cupped my hand to the water's edge and sprinkled his face, hoping he'd wake from the shock of it. "Come on, Bryce! Please, wake up."

More water. More shaking. Anything to wake him up.

My relief turned back into fear the longer he lay there. Panic twisted my chest as the seconds led to minutes, and he still didn't move.

Chapter 20

Bryce

How could I be gone if I *knew* I was gone? As soon as the darkness sucked me under, I felt like I was being turned inside out. My real self, the one on the inside, was coming out. Complete darkness turned from midnight to indigo to slate gray and, slowly, to the light.

Around me was the same cliff I'd been climbing, the same river, the same mountains. But it all reflected a different kind of light, magnifying it all. The light shined brighter than the sun, but it didn't hurt my eyes. And I could feel it. It was softer than liquid.

Somehow, in an instant, I knew it held me together.

The light held everything together, like it made everything real and alive. So alive it pulsed faintly, like a slow heartbeat.

I remembered learning that light is a particle and a wave. But here, it was so much more. It even had a smell— like Mom's magnolias mixed with ocean spray. The light pierced through me, searching for something, but gently. I wondered what it was looking for.

I noticed my body lying at the bottom of the cliff, as if it had slipped off me and lay, face up, next to the river. That's when I heard Jack.

He was on the ledge, yelling at my body, telling me to wake up, asking me if I was all right. He scrambled down and almost fell in his haste. With a twisted look, he hung his head over me and began yelling, pushing my chest, splashing water on me. What was he trying to do?

My body was useless. I was right there with him, perfectly fine. I'd never felt so alive. But was I? Or was I dead? It didn't make any sense.

There was a whole other world wrapped up in ours, but I'd just never been able to see it before. Did that mean I was dead? A ghost? Was I stuck here or would I get another chance at life? I felt like I should be panicking, but peace filled me instead. Somehow I knew everything would be okay in the end. I just didn't know *how* it would end.

I tried to calm Jack, but he wouldn't listen or couldn't hear me. He kept on yelling and sobbing. I knelt beside him and put my arm around his shoulders, asking him to stop. As I talked to him it dawned on me—he couldn't see me or hear me or feel me. Maybe I *was* dead, a ghost to him. The thought startled me, but I still sat there with my arm hooked over his shoulder and begged him to stop crying.

Chapter 21
Jack

Bryce's words came back to me then.

I had to stop and think. Stop and figure out what to do next.

I took a deep breath and held it to slow my breathing, realizing I needed to get Bryce out of the gorge. If I waited for him to wake up, who knew when we'd get out of there.

To keep myself from totally freaking out, I unpacked the first aid kit. I slid Bryce, inch by inch, out of the bush and onto my lap. I didn't want to hurt him more than he already was, but I couldn't leave him jumbled in the bush. I bandaged a couple of minor cuts and found a gash near his ankle. At the sight of fresh blood, I gulped back a surge of nausea. I told myself to stay strong.

I washed the cut and wrapped it tight to stop the bleeding. Other than that, I couldn't see any sign of serious injury.

"Bryce," I spoke urgently, "you'll probably wake up in a few minutes and be fine. I know you banged your head pretty hard, but you look good. How do you feel?" I paused as if his eyes would fly open and he'd answer me at any moment. When he didn't respond with even a flinch or a flutter of his eyelids, I clenched my teeth, cleaned up the mess, and continued talking.

"I'm sure it hurts, but I have to get you out of here. If you could help me, even a little, I'd really appreciate it." I stuffed the first aid kit into the backpack and waited for something, anything, that would let me know he was regaining consciousness.

I thought about calling Grandpa, but I didn't want to worry him if Bryce woke up soon. And I didn't want Grandpa to know I'd let him down again.

The more I thought about it, though, the more I knew I had to call him. Bryce's life might depend on it. Maybe Grandpa could come help me, or at least tell me what to do. I turned on the walkie-talkie and pushed the call button which would send a shrill buzzing on his end.

"Hello! Grandpa. Are you there?" Listening into the speaker, I waited for a reply. "It's me, Jack."

Ten seconds passed, and I pushed the call button again. Fifteen seconds. I pushed it over and over, trying to get his attention.

"Grandpa, this is Jack. Do you read me?" No answer. "Grandpa, come in. Are you there? We're in trouble. I need to talk to you."

Only static fizzed back in reply.

After several more minutes of trying to reach Grandpa, my panic turned into frustration of not knowing what to do. I couldn't figure out a way to get Bryce back to the cabin. I just wanted him to wake up.

I looked straight up the rock wall and tried to think of a way to tie Bryce in the rope to hoist him up. Maybe I could make a pulley system, but I couldn't think of a way to do it without hurting him. And it was really high up there, maybe fifty feet or more. Plus, going that way would be the long way back to the cabin. Without a trail, I might get lost or run into worse terrain.

I considered how some Native Americans made sleds out of branches and animal skins. Maybe I could lay Bryce on the poncho and drag him out. But one look down the river reminded me of why we were rock-climbing in the first place.

Luckily, he landed on a dry patch and not in the river. I shuddered to think of how that would have ended.

Maybe I could haul him out on my back. I would need my hands to climb though. I coiled the rope up and packed only what I absolutely needed into my backpack: the water bottle, walkie-talkie, first aid kit, Bryce's camera, and the fish. I left everything else next to the bush. I put my backpack on the front of my chest and shoved my arms through the straps. That way, my hands were free, and I could carry Bryce on my back.

I turned Bryce on his side and lay down next to him with my back to his stomach. Then, I rolled over to my stomach with him on top of me. The backpack dug into my chest until I pushed up onto my hands and knees with

Bryce on my back, his arms and legs hanging on either side of me.

I flung the rope over both of our backs and wound it around my torso, over my shoulders, and even through our legs, over and over again, to secure him. Finally, I tied the rope in a series of sloppy knots across the backpack on my chest. Struggling to stand on the uneven ground, I crawled to the rock wall and used it to steady myself under Bryce's dead—*No! Not dead*—weight. He was still alive, and I was determined to get him out alive.

Excruciatingly, I worked my way along the cliff bottom, foot by foot, searching for handholds or footholds to grasp. It was the only way out. I didn't want to risk climbing higher and getting stuck.

My heart raced as water splashed up and soaked my pant legs, reminding me of our impending deaths if I slipped.

As I inched my way along, I started to doubt my strength to get both of us out alive. I looked ahead to the next dry spot where I could rest.

"Hang on, Bryce, it's going to be okay," I pleaded, more to myself than to him, trying to stay strong. If I let myself panic, things wouldn't end well.

I searched for something to hold onto before my next step. But my foot slipped down the steep bank. I wobbled on a boulder at the river's edge. The rock sank into the water and I knew it was the end. I was going under. "Nooo!" My chest landed with a thud on the bank.

But the rock stopped, jarring me. A yelp shot out of my lungs, calling for help where there was none. I was wet up to my knees, but the rock held my weight and kept me from going all the way in. I clawed at the collapsing bank, desperate for something firm to grasp before the water engulfed me. My other foot found a sturdy rock, and I was able to regain my balance. I threw my body toward the cliff as adrenaline surged through me.

After a few moments of catching my breath, I readjusted Bryce and tightened the rope before moving on.

The gravelly embankment made each step seem like I was sliding on marbles. I clutched the rock wall with both hands where dry land disappeared. It was a good thing Bryce was so scrawny, because he felt heavier with every step I took. My legs trembled and buckled for a split second, making me slip and teeter toward the river again. I twisted around to grab hold of the branches of a lone bush growing impossibly in the rocks.

Leaning forward, I lay my head against an outcropping in the cliff. I didn't care about the sharp rocks or dirt pressing against my cheek. I needed to rest for just a moment.

I remembered what Dad had told me once when he was teaching us to rock climb. I'd been stuck under an overhang and felt panicky. I told Dad I couldn't do it, that I didn't have enough strength to climb out.

Dad had been belaying the rope and yelled, "Son, listen to me! When you think you're out of strength, you actually have fifty percent left. Did you know that? You've got fifty percent left, son! You can do it!" His words echoed within me as clear as if he had been standing beside me right then.

I hoped what Dad said was true. That I really did have half of my strength left. It had given me the courage to climb out of my predicament then. Now I needed the same boost, because I was sure I couldn't put one foot in front of the other for much longer.

Chapter 22

Jack

I wiped trails of sweat dripping down my face, took a drink, and pushed Bryce higher onto my back. Somehow, I managed to stand up while leaning into the cliff. I made sure my legs wouldn't give out before I took a step, and then another. Maybe there *was* an ounce of energy left in me.

I tried calling Grandpa again. "Grandpa, come in. Can you hear me?"

Nothing. No answer. Had he gone for a walk? Was he sleeping? Or maybe the walkie-talkie wasn't working. I tried different channels and called several more times as I kept hiking, getting closer to the cabin.

Maybe Bryce would wake up soon and be totally fine. We could pretend the whole accident never happened. Like it had all been a twisted dream. I dreaded showing up at the cabin. I didn't want to see the look in Grandpa's eyes when he saw what I'd done. Or not done.

I couldn't even begin to think about letting Mom down. She was already sad enough. I wondered if it was my fault because I was such a failure at home. I knew she loved me, of course, but I was never good enough to make her happy.

Dad was another story. When I was younger I liked Dad's attention, but after a while, I assumed he was ashamed of me because he was always bragging about me. It was like, for him to be proud of me, I had to sound bigger, better, and smarter than I really was.

At Dad's business party, he introduced us to his boss and said I was the starting varsity quarterback and had led our team to a winning season. In truth, I was a backup quarterback on my eighth grade team, but I rarely ever started, and it sure wasn't anything close to the high school varsity team like he led them to believe. And our team went five and four. Sure, it was a winning season, but nothing to brag about. I figured Dad was ashamed of me so he made up stories to make me seem better than I was.

People probably assumed I was the golden child, being the oldest. But no. Bryce was. Everyone knew it too. He was untouchable.

I was the failure.

And I was about to prove to all of them exactly how true that was.

Chapter 23

Bryce

I wondered why Jack kept carrying my body. I wanted to tell him it wasn't worth the struggle; I'd never been better. The more I tried to talk to him the more I realized he couldn't hear me. My words and concern couldn't help him now. I looked around to see if there was something else I could do to help, but the light around me tugged me away from the scene. He was on his own, but not alone. Something, maybe someone, was drawing me further on, away from Jack. I had to find out what it was.

The light washed a sense of acceptance over me, like arms open wide for a welcoming hug. It brought a flash of Mom and her love, only bigger, deeper, wider. My soul ached to think of her, not knowing if I'd ever see her again.

But I kept moving toward the source of the light as it drew me into a long gray tunnel. I began to understand there was more to my life than the one I was leaving behind on earth.

Chapter 24
Jack

What purpose was there in life? I wasn't good at anything. I only disappointed the people that mattered the most. If I'd been the one who fell, I sure wouldn't want this to be my end—with all of my worst life-moments hanging over my head. I wanted my life to be more meaningful and have a purpose that mattered.

"Bryce, if you can hear me, please listen." I plodded on, now past the worst of the nearly vertical canyon walls. More and more, the river gave way to dry land for me to hike on. "I'm sorry I've been such a jerk to you. I'm trying to get us out of here. I really am. And I want you to know I'm sorry for everything."

I climbed along the last tight section where the river butted up to the cliff as the setting sun cast an unearthly pink and orange glow over the valley. When I finally crossed the stepping-stones over the stream, both relief and dread filled me. I couldn't believe I made it. But Bryce hadn't stirred once that I could tell. I was afraid he hadn't survived the rough journey and that I'd made things worse.

My hand trembled as I turned the handle to the cabin door. "Grandpa!" The near darkness inside engulfed me. I stumbled to the couch, knelt on my hands and knees, and with one hand untied the rope from my chest. I leaned over to roll Bryce onto the couch, and then, I collapsed onto the cool wood floor.

Tears of relief wet my eyelashes, but I was too exhausted to cry them out. Every last thread of energy, every thought, every emotion, was gone. I closed my eyes, ready for sleep, when suddenly a door latch clicked. I jolted up.

Grandpa rushed to Bryce and me. "Jack! What happened?" He laid a hand on each of us.

I looked into his eyes, searching for some sign of understanding. But of course he didn't understand. Not yet. Maybe not ever. "He fell. I . . . I'm so sorry." I choked on the words.

Worried Bryce hadn't made it, I slid my hand on his neck where I'd found his pulse the first time. I lowered my head and closed my eyes, not yet willing to meet Grandpa's searching gaze.

Bryce's heartbeat thrummed so faintly. I couldn't be sure it was actually there. Grandpa felt Bryce's forehead like Mom would. I touched it too. He felt warm to me, not cold, like a corpse. The horrifying thought flew through my mind. I shook my head, flinging the image away.

Grandpa grimaced. "Tell me what happened."

"I . . . I don't know," I said, compiling the events in my mind.

"I know . . . you're scared. Just start with the facts."

"I'm so sorry. He was following me on the cliffs along the river because the trail is washed out. He got stuck. He panicked. I wasn't close enough to help him." I rubbed my eyes and forehead, not wanting to replay his fall in my mind.

A headache pounded away at my attempts to put two clear thoughts together. Mom always told me to drink water whenever I had a headache. It made me wonder how bad of a headache Bryce had.

"Did he ever regain consciousness?" Grandpa asked.

I hung my head and shook it slowly.

"Well, we have to get him some help." Grandpa rose to get the big first aid kit out of the pantry. He smashed an instant ice pack and cracked open smelling salts. He waved them under Bryce's nose.

"This might wake him up." Grandpa felt behind Bryce's head at the same time.

I thought I saw Bryce's eyes flicker for a second, but it must have only been my imagination or the light. He didn't move again.

"That can't be good," I said. My heart sank. What would it take to bring him back?

Grandpa pressed his lips together, sighed deeply, and put the ice pack behind Bryce's head. "We need to get him to the hospital."

"Yeah. But how?" I asked.

"I wish we could carry him out now and take him back to town for help, but we'd be stupid to hike out at night."

"Maybe he'll wake up in a little while." I shrugged and added in a whisper, "Dad's gonna kill me."

Grandpa didn't answer, confirming my worry. "Let's get something to eat, pack up, and go to bed early so we can leave at first light. I'll keep calling out on the walkie-talkie in case someone's out there."

I stared at Bryce a moment more and nodded. At least we had a plan. There wasn't much else we could do.

I took the fish out of my backpack and opened the last can of food—the baked beans—and dug in after I spooned out half for Grandpa. It made me wonder how hungry Bryce probably was, especially after he'd been so sick that morning. How long could he last without eating? Or drinking?

"Grandpa, he needs water."

"True." He nodded and thought for a minute. "We have to be careful not to get water in his lungs."

I got my canteen, and Grandpa tipped Bryce's head to the side while I poured the tiniest stream of water into his cheek, but it just dribbled out and down the couch. After a few unsuccessful tries, we soaked a clean rag and squeezed out one drop of water at a time into his mouth. I wet his lips and wiped his face. Getting water into his body was going to be a challenge. I was sure, at any minute, he would either wake up or die. I just wasn't sure which one it would be.

Grandpa lit the fire and cooked the fish whole to save time, while I kept sponging drops of water into Bryce. Despite the worry filling me, I forced myself to eat. The fish probably tasted good, but I couldn't think about anything but my brother.

"Bryce, you have to drink some water. We'll get you

out of here, okay? If you can hear me, squeeze my hand." I closed my eyes while holding his hand, waiting for him to respond, but he didn't move. "Squeeze my hand," I urged again, more insistent. Exhausted and waiting for some signal from him, I laid my head beside his on the couch and closed my eyes.

Some time later, I startled awake. How long had I been asleep? I shivered and noticed the fire had died down to a few glowing embers. A sleeping bag covered me. But I sensed something else had woken me up.

Bits and pieces of a recurring dream flashed through my mind like an old-fashioned movie reel. Grandpa holding a baby. Mom crying and chasing someone she couldn't find. She was running frantically down a bright, white hall. Dad was angry. At her? Or at me? I couldn't tell. I shook off the images—they made no sense. They never did. I checked Bryce's breathing and pulse.

Moments passed, and I couldn't feel the comforting tempo. I had done it. I had fallen asleep while my brother died. Just like I'd fallen asleep on him the other night when I was supposed to be keeping watch at the campsite. I pulled at my hair in agony. I didn't know how I'd live knowing I had caused my own brother's death. But just as I was about to give into hopelessness, I felt his pulse on his neck. Sure and steady.

It made me wonder where he was or if he was aware of what was going on? Was his mind here with us? Or somewhere else? Or just blank? I'd always assumed we would turn into dirt when we die. Like, that's it. But I wasn't so sure anymore. I couldn't believe Bryce's life was worth only a pile of dirt in the end. But that wasn't true at all. His life was worth so much more to me. To all of us.

Out the window, the darkness hung heavy, moonless, and deeply depressing. The insignificant orange glow from the fireplace didn't help one bit.

Suddenly, lightning blazed the room to life, and thunder cracked immediately behind it, rattling the windows, echoing through the canyon. I peered out the window as more lightning flashed and thunder rumbled. My dream flickered on and off along with the dazzling light show. The combination sent my heart racing. If the thunder didn't wake Bryce, I wasn't sure what ever would.

Panic and desperation gripped me like an icy black hand. I wanted to crawl under the blankets with Bryce on the couch. Instead, I got in my sleeping bag on the floor next to him.

The pictures from my dream swirled through my mind. Who was Mom chasing so frantically? It made no sense. I broke into a cold sweat, nervous, afraid.

Thunder rippled, sending gales of rain splattering onto the roof. I barely slept at all the rest of the night between the lightning and thunder, worry for Bryce, and the flashes of my dream.

Chapter 25
Jack

Gray morning light spread through the steady stream of rain. It slid down the window pane, blurring the trees outside. The window Grandpa had fixed was leaking, so I mopped up the mess and stuffed a towel around it. Whiffs of vapor puffed from my mouth, and I shivered.

Bryce was covered with his sleeping bag and all the extra blankets and coats we had. I felt his arms and forehead to make sure he was warm enough. My hands felt cold compared to him. After a moment, I could feel his slow, faint heartbeat again and relief rushed through me. He'd made it through the night.

I pushed my hunger aside to start a fire and tiptoed to

the bedroom to see if Grandpa was awake. He was already up and packing his backpack.

"Any change?" he asked.

I shook my head.

"I'm not sure about this storm," he said. "I hope it passes soon so we can leave."

I dripped water into Bryce's mouth for a while. Then I poured myself some Froot Loops and flipped through Grandpa's journal lying on the table. Dried flower petals fluttered from one of the pages. "Where did these come from?"

He shrugged and his eyes shifted. "Uh . . . your grandma was always picking flowers up here. I'm sure they were from one of our hikes or something."

I looked away at his apparent uneasiness and read the next entry which was written by Grandma, *We had the most delicious dinner of rabbit, trout, wild mushrooms, and onions. All from our own land! I could live here for the rest of my life . . .*

I never really knew Grandma. She died when I was little, but for the first time, I felt really sad that she was gone. "Tell me about her." I put my finger in the journal to hold my place.

"Hmm?" asked Grandpa as he took a bite of Froot Loops.

"About Grandma. I don't really remember her."

Grandpa sighed deeply. "She was beautiful and gracious and a spitfire from the moment I met her until the day she died."

I set the journal down.

Grandpa continued. "One time, soon after we were married, she took in a neighbor kid whose parents died.

He was eighteen, so he was old enough to be on his own, but he wasn't ready. Your Grandma let him stay with us for a few months while she taught him how to cook and clean and save money. She helped him find his first job and then shooed him out of the house as soon as he had enough saved up for a few months' rent."

"Wow. That's cool. Did you keep in touch with him?"

"For a while, but then he moved away and started a family. He sends Christmas cards now."

"How did Grandma pass away?" I asked. I'd heard she had a heart attack but didn't know the details.

Grandpa squinted like he was trying to squeeze out the pain of missing her.

"She had a massive heart attack one afternoon when she was home alone. I'd insisted on going fishing that morning even though she said she wasn't feeling good. I wasn't home to help her, or call 911, or anything. She died alone." He folded his arms across his broad chest, turned away from me, and went into his room.

I didn't know what to say. All the words I could think of seemed irrelevant, so I didn't say anything. Instead, I flipped through a few more pages of the journal. Nothing caught my eye until the second-to-last page.

To Do:

~~*Fix bedroom window*~~
Clean out fireplace and flue
~~*Build a trunk for the bedroom*~~
~~*Sew new curtains*~~
Repair shingles
Dreams:
Build a windmill or waterwheel for power.

Camp under the stars at the lake with Jack and Bryce.
~~Live at the cabin for a summer.~~
~~Hunt a bear—bear skin rug for the cabin fireplace.~~
Family reunion here with our kids and grandkids.

I watched the rain out the window and wondered if Grandpa would get to live out all of his dreams and if I could help him somehow. I didn't realize he was lonely and missing Grandma so much.

His lists made me think about my own dreams. But I wasn't sure if I had any. At home, life was the same every day with school, homework, football, and chores. The same things over and over. It all felt so purposeless. I guess I'd forgotten to dream in the middle of it all. I didn't know *what* I would dream about now, other than Bryce waking up and being well.

I flipped through a few pages and tore out a blank one. I wrote *My Dreams* on the top and stared at the fire for a moment before writing *Become a sheriff*, but immediately, I scratched it out. It was what I wanted to be someday, not really a dream. It was just something I figured I might be good at, and it wouldn't be too hard to learn how to do.

I got up, opened the door, and peered through the rain at the green pine trees and aspen leaves framed by the dark gray sky. Time seemed to stand still. Papery white aspen bark offset the charcoal-black knots in the trees. Deer tracks lay scattered in the mud.

Guilt thumped into my chest again. How had I gotten so deep into trouble? More than trouble. It didn't matter what consequences would be handed out to me as a result of not protecting Bryce. The worst consequence of all would be his life.

I knelt beside the couch and asked, "Bryce, can you hear me?" His chest rose and fell, and I squeezed his arm. "Listen to me. You have to wake up."

My pleading soon turned into a confession. I whispered in his ear, "I need you, Bryce . . . Mom needs you. So does Dad. I know I've been selfish and . . . and mean. I didn't care about anyone but myself. I didn't think I cared about you . . . but that's not true." I kept on talking. Maybe I could revive him by sheer willpower.

Chapter 26
Bryce

Even though I'd never really known her, I recognized Grandma right away. It wasn't just her red hair that I'd seen in pictures, but her warm smile and shining green eyes drew me in. She belonged to me. Or, rather, I belonged to her.

She opened one arm to me. I stepped toward her, wanting to feel her embrace, but something stopped me. I looked down at a tiny baby in her other arm. Somehow the baby seemed familiar too, even though I was sure I'd never seen him before.

About to ask Grandma who he was, I heard my name being called in the distance. It sounded urgent, panicked.

I didn't like the sound of it. It didn't fit in with the peace around me. I moved closer to Grandma, trying to ignore it.

"Bryce," she said in a voice as sweet as spring flowers. "You're so handsome. How I've missed watching you grow up."

A hundred questions filled me. "Where are we, Grandma? What is this place?" I looked around. She was sitting in a rocking chair in some sort of parlor or sitting room. It looked ornate, decorated with gold and white furniture that Mom would never let me touch if she were here, but it felt cozy and welcoming. "Can I stay here with you?"

She smiled and shook her head. "Not this time, Bryce. Go back and tell your family that I'm here and so is William." She looked down at the baby she was holding, and his blue-green eyes startled me. Had I seen them before? Grandma continued, "Tell them I'm watching over him and he's absolutely perfect. Tell your grandfather I miss him and love him, and I'm waiting for him. He's not to blame. Make sure you tell him that, Bryce. He's not to blame. Can you remember that?"

I nodded, but I didn't want to return home. There was too much sadness there. Too many problems. Life would be so much easier here. "Why can't I stay with you, Grandma?" I looked at the baby, still wondering who he was.

"It's not your time yet, my dear. You have to be with your family. They desperately need you. You have a mission to go back to them. You have to help them understand and remember."

"Remember what?"

She looked down at the baby. "Help your mom and dad remember that they love each other."

"Oh," I replied, thinking back to the pictures I'd found of them looking like they'd been in love.

"And help Jack remember his—" Grandma stopped and looked over her shoulder at a deep, rumbling voice, but I couldn't make out the words.

"Help Jack remember what?" I asked, straining to see what she was looking at.

She shook her head. "It's time for you to go now. Time to go home."

"But *this* feels like home," I protested and reached out to her again. "And how will I know how to help my family anyway?"

"You'll know. Remember to tell them I love them, and that Grandpa's not to blame." She smiled so deeply that I ached to stay with her forever.

Chapter 27

Jack

The thunderstorm wasn't slowing down.

"I think I should go," Grandpa said.

"What?"

"I'll hike out by myself and get help. You stay here with your brother. We can't take him out in that downpour."

The thought of being alone up here with Bryce struck fear in my heart. What if Bryce got worse or died while Grandpa was gone? What if something else happened and I didn't know what to do? The bear could break down the door or those strangers could come back. What if something happened to Grandpa, and I was stuck up here forever?

But neither of us could think of another solution.

I helped Grandpa finish packing. We walked out into the rain and downriver a short way. Grandpa turned and looked intently into my eyes. "Please stay safe. Keep taking care of Bryce. You're doing a fine job." Raindrops were flooding his eyes. Or were they tears? "I love you. You can do this. I want you to know that."

I shook his hand as a promise to take care of Bryce and nearly cried myself. I didn't want Grandpa to leave us alone, but I knew there was no other way.

He turned once more, gave me a hug, and said, "Stay away from the river in case there's a flash flood."

Great. One more thing to worry about. I nodded and waved. "Bye, Grandpa. Love you, too."

By noon, the rain had only intensified. I was restless and nervous about Grandpa being out on his own. It was a long hike back, at least six hours. I hoped his knee would hold up and the rain would keep the wild animals snug in their own hiding places and not stalking Grandpa.

A few hours later, the sun had set. The darkness made the cabin close in on me. I was going stir-crazy. I needed something to do to keep myself from worrying so much. I restarted the fire and boiled noodles for dinner. Then I had to get more water.

On the way to the stream, I checked the traps. The second one had a mouse in it, squirming—not fully dead. The way it squealed and flopped around made me sick. It reminded me of Bryce's fall. How he seemed to bounce when he hit the ground. I worked to untangle the mouse from the wire, pushed back my gag reflex, and let it go.

Despair settled in my heart along with the darkness of the storm. I didn't know what else I could do to help Bryce.

If only I could turn back time so the climb, or actually the whole trip, had happened differently. If I hadn't been trying to show off to Bryce at the river on the first day of our trip, none of this would have happened. I should have been a better brother to Bryce in the first place. And now it might be too late.

Stinging regret shot through me. With anger, I shoved my fist into the air and crouched down, ready to crumple into the pine needles below me. I spoke aloud into the cool, dark forest. "I can't do this. Someone help me." Louder, almost yelling, I called into the trees, "Someone, anyone, help us!" My desperate words faded into the wispy clouds, as feeble and insignificant as I felt.

The only reply was the humming river and the rain tumbling on the aspen leaves. I was abandoned and all alone.

As I knelt by the stream, something twinkled in the water. It mimicked the stars, so I looked up beyond the tree branches.

Through a break in the clouds, millions of stars glistened down on me. I'd never seen stars so bright or close before. It was as if I could reach up and swirl my fingers through them like water in a pond. One star shot across the opening, and I dared to make a wish. Someone to rescue Bryce and that he would live and be totally fine. Or was that three wishes? Too much to wish for?

The nearness of the stars made me hope for something, or someone, beyond myself—otherwise I really was alone. I breathed a prayer into the sky. "God, if you're there, Bryce needs your help. Please, don't let him die. Please." I didn't know what else to say. I'd never prayed before.

In the water the twinkling caught my eye again.

Tilting my head to the side, I realized I was looking straight into the eyes of a huge bullfrog. We both flinched and the frog hopped away. I remembered Mom telling me she'd eaten frog legs at a fancy restaurant once and they'd tasted like chicken.

Determined to catch it for supper, I lunged and grappled at the frog, but it hopped again, out of my reach. But its wet, slippery, wiggling body was no match for my desperation. I clamped the frog against my chest and carried it to the cabin. I was starving after not eating a decent meal for days.

My celebration was short-lived when I realized I would have to kill it. Nausea rose in my throat. I settled on using the long cooking fork in the kitchen and held the frog on a cutting board. I winced as I speared it twice in the middle of its belly. The squirming and helplessness repulsed me just as the mouse had. I had no idea if I was supposed to skin it or cook it whole.

When it was finally dead, I cooked it in the cast iron skillet using oil, salt, pepper, and other spices, the way Grandpa did with the marmot. It wasn't pretty, but I hoped it would taste as good as I was dreaming.

While it cooked, I gave Bryce more water and checked his bandaged hand. Unwrapping it, disappointment filled me at how red and swollen it looked. I should have checked it earlier. I put antibacterial salve on it and rebandaged it and his other cuts.

I checked Bryce's breathing and pulse, afraid he would die while Grandpa was gone. I rotated my jobs: check Bryce's pulse, give him water, turn the frog. It kept me busy and my mind off negative thoughts threatening to immobilize me.

Not surprisingly, the frog did taste like chicken. It was the best meal I'd eaten out here, but Bryce should have been the one eating those frog legs. He was the hunter. The one who deserved this. The frog had basically landed right in my lap. I hadn't done anything to deserve it.

I held a frog leg close to Bryce's nose, hoping the smell would wake him. "Hey, Bryce." I knelt beside him, searching his face for any sign of consciousness. "Time to eat. Grandpa hiked out to get help. He'll be back soon, and we'll get you out of here." I spoke loud and clear as if he were deaf. I hoped he could hear me, somewhere deep down inside of him. "I caught a frog. It tastes like chicken, just like Mom said." I nibbled at the frog meat. "When you wake up, you can have some, too. I saved a leg for you. And a Hershey's bar."

I finished the frog legs, sighed deeply when Bryce didn't flinch, and laid my head on the couch beside him. I put my hand on his chest, feeling its shallow rise and fall, and fell asleep.

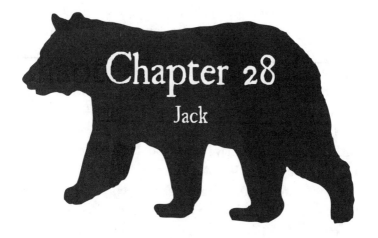

Chapter 28
Jack

In the morning, the rain had stopped. I cleaned up my mess from dinner, started the fire again, and went outside. Damp, fresh air filled my lungs and filled me with expectation.

On my way back from the outhouse, I searched through the underbrush for strawberries. I spotted something red in a bush, but they were different: small, round red berries that I knew might be poisonous. There had to be more strawberries out here somewhere. I'd been looking for several minutes when a deep sound behind me stopped me in my tracks. The whole forest listened along with me as I froze and looked through the trees toward the cabin.

"Hello?" someone called out.

Could it be? Everything in me hoped it was Bryce—alive, awake, and walking around. Or maybe it was Grandpa, back with help already.

The person moved forward.

All the hope in me dissipated. It wasn't Bryce or Grandpa.

It was that tall, lanky guy we passed on our hike the other day.

"Oh, there you are," he said, and looked to his left. From behind a wide spruce tree came the shorter, stocky man, the one who gave me the creeps. His dark eyes looked like they held secrets, one of them probably being why they broke into Grandpa's cabin. He stepped closer and lowered his eyes, sending a shiver up my spine.

The tall man held the reins of his donkey. "We thought we'd find you here," he said as he wiped sweat from his forehead with his hat.

I stood there feeling like someone shot me with a stun gun. I had to get into the cabin, but I didn't want them to know I was alone with Bryce.

"You boys all right?" he asked. "Your grandpa told us to check on you."

They were lying to me, I knew it. There's no way Grandpa would have trusted them. "We're great," I said, trying to sound calm.

"How's your brother?" the bald man asked, crossing his arms over his bulging chest.

I took a few steps closer and could see their backpacks on the ground by the porch. Were they breaking in again? I had to get them out of here somehow.

"He's good. He's coming down from the lake," I lied

again, hoping they'd leave me alone. I needed help, but not from them. They might cause more trouble, and Grandpa couldn't be too far off now.

The tall man walked closer. "That right?" He tugged at the reluctant donkey.

"Yes, sir," I answered, taking a few steps forward, hoping they'd get the hint. I was going into the cabin— without them.

He looked at me for a minute and then over my shoulder. "What's taking him so long?"

I glanced back, up the mountain, giving myself a second to come up with a convincing lie. "I ran ahead. I'm gonna start the fire for our lunch. I'd invite you, but we only have enough for the two of us." I held my breath, hoping he'd believe me.

The other man scowled and walked to his backpack. Picking it up, he said, "Let's go, Tom."

Tom nodded but didn't turn away. "You sure you're both okay?"

I nodded, not daring to say one more word for fear that I'd give myself away. I had to protect Bryce.

They gathered their packs and the donkey. "You take care, now," said the tall man. I waved and forced a smile.

I let my breath out silently and stood there until they turned and hiked downriver, out of sight. I just hoped they wouldn't give Grandpa any trouble if he ran into them on his way up.

What a close call. I'd have to keep a look out and make sure they stayed away for good and didn't return to spy on me.

Inside, I knelt beside Bryce and checked his pulse. I regretted leaving him alone for that long. Those guys could have broken into the cabin again. As soon as I scanned through my mental list of all the worst things that could have happened, I sighed when I found Bryce's slow, steady heartbeat again.

But I didn't allow myself to feel any relief until I'd given him water and started heating up some noodles over the hot coals. Staring into the short flames, my stomach twisted and growled. I dug out a spoonful of peanut butter and ate it with graham crackers and the leftover, soggy noodles.

I was worried about Grandpa. Why wasn't he back yet? What if something happened to him, or those guys got to him, and I was stranded for good?

I counted how many hours it should take a rescuer to hike up if Grandpa had made it down safely last night. I had to trust that he did. I figured a fast hiker could make it up here in six to eight hours. It was late morning, so they should be here soon if they started out early.

"Hang on, Bryce," I said. "We're getting closer to help. Just hang in there with me for a while longer. Okay?"

I planned out what I'd do if Grandpa didn't make it back by evening. Tomorrow, I'd strap Bryce on my back and hike out. I'd have to bring some kind of weapon in case I encountered a wild animal. Maybe pack one of the kitchen knives and look for a good walking stick to use as a spear.

As I looked around the cabin for what I'd need to take, a droning sound grew in the distance and slowly filled the air. I looked out the window, afraid of what it could be.

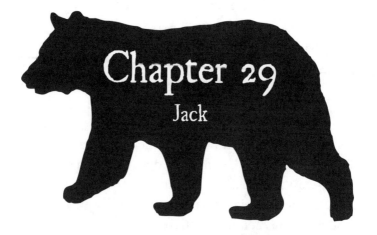

Chapter 29

Jack

I could have sworn the river was getting louder. Grandpa's warning about a flash flood rang through me. Still peering out the bedroom window, I wondered why it sounded so choppy, so close. Was the river flooding? What if it flooded the cabin? How would I get Bryce out in time and to higher ground? I raced to grab essentials to pack and unwrapped the rope to tie Bryce to my back again.

Then the sound grew louder and more distinct, like a motorcycle. Could it be an ATV? Maybe rescuers?

I ran outside and looked down the trail. The river looked normal, and I didn't see anyone coming, but the sound got louder still. Then I looked up and realized it was a helicopter. It flew above me, along the canyon. I waved and yelled and jumped up and down like a madman. Did they know where we were? Grandpa had to be with them, directing them.

The helicopter disappeared up the canyon, and my heart dropped. They'd come back, I told myself. I waited. One minute. Two minutes. Five. Ten. I turned to go back into the cabin. I'd pack up to be ready when they came back.

They're going to come back.

They have to.

But what if they didn't? How could I signal to them? Bryce probably would know how to get the helicopter's attention.

I stood on the front porch and finally heard a faint rumbling. As it got louder, the helicopter rose over the ridge to the west, like a beacon of hope.

"I'm here! I'm here!" I waved my arms and ran to the stream near a clearing. "Help!" I shouted. I knew they couldn't hear me or even see me, but it didn't matter. We were being rescued!

The helicopter hovered uphill past the timberline and didn't move. I couldn't see much of it through the trees. *What's taking them so long? Why don't they just land?*

A few minutes later, a tall, blond man in a blue jumpsuit came running toward me with what I guessed was a stretcher at his side.

"Are you Jack?" he asked.

"Yes, sir. Did you just come out of that helicopter?" I asked, astonished.

"Yes. I'm Mike. I'm a paramedic." He shook my hand .

I stared at him, speechless.

"How are you? Are you okay?"

"I'm fine," I said and shook his hand, trying to match his firm grasp.

"The pilot can't land because of the terrain. We have to get your brother in there as fast as possible."

"Yes, sir." I led him to the cabin.

"Listen, Jack. I need you to help me get your brother up the hill and hooked to a harness that will lift him into the chopper. Then you'll be next. Not scared of heights, are you?"

I shook my head. "No, sir."

"Good. Your grandpa is waiting for us at the hospital."

"Is he okay?"

"Yes. A little tired, but he's fine."

It took me a minute to comprehend what was happening and how Grandpa had already gotten to the hospital, but there was no time to lose.

"Do you understand?" Mike asked firmly.

"Yes, sir." I nodded and led him into the cabin.

Mike quickly checked Bryce's vitals, put a brace on his neck, and felt along his arms and legs. "Okay, you hold on here and slide it under him gently when I roll him to the side." While we worked to get Bryce situated and Mike strapped him on the stretcher, I kept talking to Bryce, telling him what was going on and that he'd be at the hospital soon.

On our way to the helicopter, I couldn't stop trembling because of the intensity of the noise and the nervous excitement I felt, but I did my best to help carry Bryce and support him as Mike secured the stretcher in a special harness. Slowly, Bryce rose above me and into the cavern of the helicopter where I saw arms reach out and pull him in.

A minute later, the cable was lowered again, and Mike clipped me into the harness.

"Hold on here, okay?" he yelled over the roar.

I nodded, too nervous to say anything.

"And it's best not to look down if you're nervous." He smirked.

As the cable pulled taut and lifted me off my feet, I gripped tight, my knuckles turning white. I couldn't believe what was happening. It felt like I was in a dream or a movie, only without the glamor. It was more like a horror movie. I just hoped it would have a good ending.

Chapter 30
Jack

After an exhilarating helicopter ride over the mountains, we finally arrived at the hospital. I wished I could have enjoyed the view, but I was so enthralled with what Mike and the pilot were doing that I couldn't take in anything else. As Mike was caring for Bryce, he said that Grandpa had already called my mom and dad to catch the first flight to Denver from Atlanta.

At the hospital, the paramedics raced to the helicopter, swept Bryce away, and started checking on me. I was startled at the attention. I was fine. I just wanted them to focus on Bryce.

I tried to hop out of the helicopter, but Mike grabbed

my arm. It was a good thing, because as soon as I hit the ground, my knees buckled under me. Mike lifted me up and waved a nurse over with a wheelchair. I was embarrassed, but I didn't want to cause any more problems for anyone, so I sat down. They wheeled me through the hospital and down an elevator to where Grandpa was. When I saw him, I asked the nurse if I could get up. For the second time in two days, Grandpa gave me a big bear hug.

"Thank God," he said and sighed heavily into my ear.

Grandpa and I checked in with the receptionist and leaned side-by-side in the waiting room chairs while I told him about the flight and how amazing Mike was with Bryce.

Later, orange shafts of the sunset lit up the room, and in walked the two men we'd run into on the mountain, Tom and the other guy.

"What're they doing here?" I whispered to Grandpa, nudging him.

He stood to shake their hands. "Hi, Tom. Craig." Then turning to me, Grandpa said, "They helped get me down the trail."

"What do you mean?" I asked.

"Remember how it was raining when I left?"

"Yeah." I ran my hand through my hair, confused.

"Well, it was taking me a long time to hike out because everything was so wet and slippery, and my knee wasn't doing so well. I ran into these guys and they let me ride their donkey the rest of the way."

My eyes widened. I couldn't believe it. I didn't trust those guys for one second, but Grandpa had.

"I told them what had happened and asked them to

check on you if they made it to the cabin before help came."

"Really?" I felt a sick thud in my stomach. I had totally misjudged them. And lied to them.

Grandpa thanked them and shook their hands.

"I thought you guys broke into my grandpa's cabin."

They both nodded and Tom said, "We did, but only because I got hurt, and we needed a place to rest up before moving on."

Craig spoke up then. "You shouldn't be so quick to judge."

Beads of sweat popped out on my forehead. I felt like I was turning red all over. "I'm sorry, sir. I . . . I made a mistake. I was wrong."

He nodded, and they started to turn away.

"Wait. I owe you both. How can I repay you?"

"No need," said Tom. "We happened to be in the right place at the right time and were glad to help. You're the real hero, carrying your brother to safety in the first place. Your grandpa told us what you'd done to save him."

I blinked twice. Grandpa squeezed my shoulder as the men walked down the hall and out the emergency room doors.

Hero? I was not a hero. I was a lousy brother and failure to everyone who really mattered to me. How could they think I was a hero? They didn't know the truth about how I hadn't looked out for my little brother. I had climbed too high and too fast when I knew he couldn't keep up. The word *murderer* popped in my head. I held that word out at arm's length. I couldn't call myself that, yet. I couldn't let myself believe that Bryce was going to die. I sat next to Grandpa in the waiting room and blinked my eyes against the bright lights and the thoughts buzzing around inside me. "Bryce has to survive," I said under my breath. "He has to."

Later, Grandpa slumped in his chair and snored lightly beside me. I flipped through a news magazine without really seeing it. I couldn't think about anything until I saw Bryce and knew how he was doing. The second time I asked the receptionist, she huffed and said she'd tell me as soon as she heard anything.

I was almost asleep when a nurse showed up and whispered, "Jack? They hooked your brother up to an IV to rehydrate him, and he's in stable condition. It'll be a little while longer before we can do a check-up on you. Can I get you something to drink or eat in the meantime?"

Relief flooded me to hear that Bryce was in good hands. I nodded. "Yes, ma'am. I'm starving."

She returned with a candy bar and a Sprite and said, "It's from my own lunch. Don't tell anyone." She winked. "I'll get you something else from the café in a bit."

After I ate her snack, even though it was a bunch of sugar, my adrenaline must have come to the end of itself. I couldn't keep my eyes open any longer.

I was mostly asleep when the nurse woke me again. "Jack?" She rubbed my shoulder. "Come with me."

I straightened in my chair. Leftover dread in the pit of my stomach reminded me of where I was. I wasn't in a dream. *My brother is in a coma. We're in a hospital—not at the cabin and not at home.* I rubbed away the gritty feeling in my eyes and followed the nurse.

"We'll check your vitals and make sure you're hydrated. Your grandpa told us all about your big adventure." She smiled sympathetically. She led me behind a white curtained-off area and motioned for me to sit on the bed.

"I talked to your father. He and your mom caught a flight out here. They should be here in a couple of hours."

Ugh, my parents. They were going to kill me.

The nurse stuck a clip on my finger and took my temperature and blood pressure. I was fine, of course. Maybe if something horrible had happened to me too, it would have somehow made up for Bryce's accident. But no, all I had was a cut on my leg and a couple of bruises from the river.

"Everything looks good," she said with a smile, and then she left me for a moment. She returned with a large bottle of water and a tray of assorted hospital fare: three cups of red Jell-O, a Styrofoam bowl of chicken noodle soup, a mound of saltine crackers, and an apple. "Here, eat up while I go check the next patient in. I'll be back."

She started to leave, but I stopped her. "How is he?"

"I'll have the doctor come talk to you, but they're taking real good care of him, so don't you worry. Stay positive for him, darling. He needs you." She closed the curtain and left me alone to eat.

I could hardly hold my head up long enough to take a few bites, so I lay down, thinking I'd just doze for a few minutes.

"Jack . . . Jack, wake up." Someone was tapping my shoulder. "Your mom is here."

I bolted upright. "Mom?" I must have been out for hours.

"Hi, sweetheart." Mom hugged me and held on longer than normal. "How're you holding up?"

I hesitated before I wrapped my arm around her waist and leaned into her. So she wasn't going to kill me right away. Maybe it'd be a slow, painful death instead.

"I'm fine." I looked into her blue-gray eyes. The same eyes as Bryce's that I hoped I'd get to see again. "Have you seen him?"

She nodded, looked down, and then sat in the chair across from me. She pulled her brown hair into a ponytail. Dark pits under her red-rimmed eyes made her look sadder than normal.

"Is he gonna be okay?" I asked.

"They don't know yet," she said with a sigh. "They've been rehydrating him and doing some tests to see what part of his brain has been affected. We'll know more when the MRI results come back. But he hasn't shown any sign of consciousness yet."

I rubbed my face. "If he doesn't make it . . . I . . . I don't know . . ." I couldn't finish my sentence.

"He'll make it, Jack. He has to." The determination in her voice made me half-believe her. "It's not his time to go. He'll come back to us."

"But what if he doesn't?" I said, suddenly angry. "What if he dies? Or what if he lives, but never wakes up?"

"Don't talk like that," Mom gently reprimanded me. "We have to think positive thoughts for him."

"What good'll that do?"

She sighed again, stretching her neck from side to side.

"Dad's probably gonna kill me, huh?"

"No, sweetheart, Dad loves you. The most important thing right now is not who's right or wrong . . . nobody is to blame." She smiled, but her eyes looked sad. "The most important things are that you're okay and that we all help Bryce get better."

I nodded, hugged her again, and said, "You know

when I yelled at you a few weeks ago about that project I had to do for school, and I slammed the door in your face?"

She nodded.

"I'm really sorry I did that."

"We'll get through this," she whispered and hugged me again.

The nurse walked in. "Mrs. Harrison?"

Mom wiped her eyes and answered, "Yes, ma'am?"

"Just checking in on Jack. Are you doing well? Is there anything either of you need?"

"Can I see my brother?" I asked.

"Sure. Follow me." She held the curtains open for us and led us up an elevator and through a maze of whitewashed halls. I was disoriented as we turned left, then right, and then left again. I'd never be able to find my way out of here alone.

We came to a set of double doors and the nurse swiped a badge to open them. We walked past a reception desk and several private rooms, turned a corner, and entered room number 365. The nurse knocked lightly and announced herself. At first no one responded, but then Dad peeked out from behind the curtain.

"Oh, there you are." He sounded anxious but relieved at the same time.

"Jack's vitals are all good," Mom whispered to Dad. "How's Bryce? Any change?"

Dad shook his head and pursed his lips. "You all right, son?"

I nodded, waiting for his lecture or the consequences he was sure to dole out.

He stood and looked at me like he was trying hard

not to say anything. I couldn't tell if he was so angry and disappointed that he couldn't put the words together or what. "Can I see him, Dad?"

He tipped his head toward Bryce. "Come on."

The lights were dim and, aside from the heart monitor beeping, all was silent. Eerily silent. Mom and Dad stood beside the bed as I sat on the edge next to Bryce. I searched his face, wondering where my brother really was and why he hadn't woken up yet.

"Hey, Bryce, it's me. They have you in this great hospital. You've got lots of water and medicine now. They'll take good care of you. You can open your eyes anytime, and let us know you're all right." I reached out and fist-bumped his shoulder, barely touching him.

"You're missing out on the Jell-O," I continued. "It's the only good food here. But when you get out I'll buy you a Slurpee at 7–Eleven. You can get the biggest one you want and fill it with every flavor they have, just how you like it." I pulled a chair close to his bed.

"So tell us what happened, Jack," Dad said.

"Grandpa and the nurses already filled us in, Marcus," Mom said, nudging Dad.

"Yes, I know," he said. "But I want to know what really happened. Why did Bryce fall? How could you have let him fall?"

There it was. Dad did blame me.

"It wasn't my fault, Dad. I swear. I tried to help him, but he was too far away, and I didn't know what to do."

Fear struck through me like a lightning bolt as I replayed the events for them. Dad's silence didn't help.

"Maybe I should've let Bryce lead. He might have found an easier route for himself," I spoke more to myself than to Mom and Dad. "Maybe it was my fault."

"We're not here to blame anyone," Mom said, playing the go-between. "We just want to know what happened. And we're proud of you for getting him to the cabin. Grandpa told us what a journey you made to get him to safety."

Dad nodded but still didn't say anything.

I stared at him, not sure what to say.

"Dad, please don't be mad," I begged. "I'll do anything to make it better." But I knew nothing could make it better for any of us unless Bryce woke up and was well.

Dad clenched his jaw, looked at Mom, and shifted his gaze to me. "I know, son. Me too." He sighed deeply. "Me too."

Mom and Dad left to get a bite to eat. I pulled a chair next to Bryce and laid my head on his bed, falling into a troubled sleep. Hushed voices kept pulling me in and out of consciousness.

". . . a TBI or traumatic brain injury . . . long-term effects," said a man's voice. ". . . fracture to the skull . . . significant brain swelling . . . prevents blood flow . . . loss of oxygen . . ."

Mom asked, "What if he doesn't wake up?"

". . . reduce swelling . . . three days, hopefully . . . ," answered the man who must have been the doctor.

Dad asked, "What if he does wake up?"

All I wanted was to sleep and for the voices to stop and let me be. Let me drift off into black forgetfulness.

". . . stabilize him and . . . options of therapies . . . ," continued the man's voice.

"Does he have any other broken bones or internal injuries?" asked Mom.

". . . sprained ankle . . . broken ribs," he answered.

Someone nudged me. "Jack." It was Mom. "Jack, come lie down." She led me to a cot. In a haze of confusion, I curled up without a word. A blanket covered me, and a pillow slid under my head.

In my dream, Bryce stood there smiling and happy one minute. The next, he was falling into a massive, dark hole so far down that I couldn't see the bottom. I reached out to him in the dream, trying to catch him, stop him from falling. All the while, he grinned unevenly, his unnatural look haunting me.

Chapter 31
Bryce

I didn't want to go back. Life on earth was plain-old hard compared to where I was with Grandma.

"It's time, Bryce," said Grandma. "They need you."

"Why did you bring me here if I just have to go back?" I asked, wanting to walk past her and farther into what seemed like a mansion. What was in there? Who was in there?

"I didn't bring you here," she said with a smirk.

"Well, whoever did isn't funny at all."

"It's not a joke, Bryce. And maybe you weren't brought here for *you*. Maybe you're here for someone else." She smiled and rocked the baby in her arms. "But in the end, it's your choice if you want to stay here or go back."

"It is?" I didn't realize I had a choice in the matter. If I stayed, I'd live forever in peace. If I went back, I'd have a lifetime of . . . life. Regular, sometimes boring, sometimes exciting, life. Did my family really need me? Grandma seemed to think so. I wondered what would happen to them if I didn't go back. How would Mom and Dad handle losing me? And what about Jack? I knew he was dying inside from the guilt of letting me fall.

A frantic voice behind me, below me, still called my name and begged me to go back. I couldn't ignore it. Somebody needed me. I had to return home.

I reached out and touched Grandma's fingertips for a moment that seemed to last forever. I fought the urge to grab onto her hand and stay. I forced myself to back away through the thick light. It was even harder to go when I started to hear the persistent voices in the background. I looked at Grandma's red hair and smiling green eyes until I couldn't see her anymore.

I was in a dark tunnel that pressed in on me, suffocated me. I felt like I was going to die all over again. I resisted the pressure as a deep voice resonated within me, "You aren't alone. Don't be afraid. I'm always with you."

I wasn't alone on my journey. Never was. Never will be. Now I understood why I had to go. I had to tell Jack. He needed to know there was more to our lives and that he wasn't alone. I stepped toward the tunnel, in it, and passed through it, much too slowly, until I reached the other side.

I turned back and looked at the light as it receded, twinkling alive like a star. It moved farther and farther away until it was only a pinprick. I didn't blink until it disappeared.

Suddenly, another light replaced it, harsh and uninviting. I squeezed my eyes shut. The contrast shocked me. I didn't dare breathe.

Then I heard a long, disturbing *beeeeeeeeeeeeeeeeeeep*.

As I watched from above my body, people ran around me, madly, frantically, holding metal plates, pressing them to my chest. I choked on a breath and tried to scream for them to stop. I was being torn back into my body. Then an electric jolt zapped me and forced me to look up at the awful light, even though what I really hoped to see were Grandma's eyes.

As I focused past the light, I saw hands and faces above me, leaning in, hovering.

What are they doing? I wondered. *Trying to save me? Fix me? They need to stop. They must not realize I'm right here.*

I'm already saved.

Already fixed.

The beeping finally quieted and so did all the people. They stopped moving and racing around and simply stared at me.

What are they doing?

Waiting?

Watching?

Hoping?

Chapter 32

Jack

I was still sleeping when the beeping started. In my dream, Bryce smiled a quirky but warm smile. He looked deep into my eyes and said, "I'm right here. You're not alone."

The beeping broke the comfort of my dream. I sat up and saw nurses and a doctor rush in to resuscitate Bryce. What took maybe sixty seconds felt like an hour. I groaned as they worked to force him back to life.

Mom ran into the room. A nurse reached out and held her back while she searched their faces for an explanation. I couldn't look at her. My own panic was too much to handle. I couldn't deal with hers too.

I prayed for the second time in my life: "God, if you're there, bring Bryce back to us. Please, bring him back. Don't let him go."

When the long beeping stopped, I continued whispering "please" over and over again.

Mom covered her mouth with one hand and grabbed my hand with the other, squeezing the life out of it.

"Mom, ow," I said softly. I readjusted my hand and held hers in both of mine. "Where's Dad?" I asked.

"At Grandpa's. I told him to go home to sleep."

Everyone stood still in the room. No one dared to breathe, as if it would suck any remaining air out of Bryce.

We all watched.

Waited.

Doubted.

Mom broke the silence. "Is he . . . is he okay?"

I stood up. Mom walked to Bryce's side. Everyone stood frozen, eyes popped open wide.

All of them.

Including Bryce's.

Chapter 33

Jack

Bryce blinked at the circle of faces above him, and then he turned his head to the side, and his gaze focused on me. A slow smile grew on his face. He opened his mouth to speak, but an oxygen mask covered his mouth. Someone, a nurse, helped him pull it off.

"Jack," said Bryce, his voice raw and hoarse.

I stood silently, unbelieving, blinking back at my little brother.

Mom knelt at Bryce's side as the nurses stepped back. "Bryce, you're awake!" She held his face and kissed his forehead.

"Mom." He turned his head to her. "Why are you crying?"

Tears rolled down her cheeks as she hugged him, put her face beside his, and breathed in deeply through her nose. Maybe smelling him like a mother bear does to her cub.

A hushed silence fell over the room. I was stunned. Mom pulled away and wiped her eyes. The doctor asked Bryce a few simple questions.

"What's your name?"

"Bryce. Bryce Lee Harrison." Bryce tilted his head toward the doctor.

"Do you know what year it is?"

"Two-k-sixteen." Bryce raised an eyebrow.

"How old are you?"

"Twelve." Bryce frowned and said, "Can I ask you a question?"

"Sure," said the doctor with a smirk.

"Where am I?"

"You're in the hospital, in Ft. Collins. You fell and hit your head, and you've been unconscious for a couple of days. How do you feel?"

"I . . . I feel okay." He scrunched his nose. "I have a bad headache though."

"Of course," said the doctor. "We'll increase your medicine." He nodded toward a nurse, and she hurried out of the room.

Dad rushed into the room, looking around at everyone and then down at Bryce. "Is that you, Bryce?" His jaw dropped, and he touched Bryce's face.

"Hi, Dad. Yes, it's me. Why wouldn't it be?"

"You gave us such a scare. We didn't know if you'd make it," Dad explained.

Bryce knit his eyebrows together and looked at Dad and then Mom.

The doctor cleared his throat and asked, "Can I speak to you alone, Mr. and Mrs. Harrison?"

Mom and Dad exchanged their own worrisome glances and followed the doctor into the hall. Another nurse busied herself taking Bryce's vitals and then excused herself also.

"Jack, what did Dad mean?" asked Bryce, searching my eyes.

"About what?"

"When he said he wasn't sure if I'd make it." He tried to sit up but winced and lay down again. "Did I almost die?" he asked.

I helped him find the controls and pushed a button to move the bed into a sitting position. "We weren't sure," I began. "You fell when we were rock climbing and you've been unconscious until now."

"How long was I out?"

"About two days." I sat down in the chair beside him.

"Only two?" Bryce looked up at the ceiling and shut one eye like he was counting the days. "Huh. It seemed like I was up there for . . . forever."

"What do you mean—up there?" I followed Bryce's gaze to the ceiling. *He was up where? Where does he think he went? On the ceiling?*

The nurse walked in, gave Bryce his medicine, and asked him if he needed anything else.

"No, thank you, not right now," Bryce said.

"Your parents will be back in a minute. They're discussing your recovery with the doctor," she said and walked out.

"What do you mean, you were up there?" I pointed upward.

"When I fell, my body was here, on earth, but I went to . . . to heaven, I guess. I don't know how it happened."

I narrowed my eyes. Maybe the doctor gave him some drugs that were making him imagine things.

"What?" Bryce asked. "You don't believe me?"

I shook my head. "Hmm . . . I just don't get it."

"I was there. I remember everything about it."

"It's okay. It was just a dream. I had a few strange dreams myself the past two nights."

"It wasn't a dream," he insisted. "Not at all." Agitated, he readjusted the bed's position, cringing again at the pain.

"Settle down. We can talk about it later. Just rest, for now." I stood up and fidgeted. "You need to get better so we can get you out of here soon and go home. Back to our normal lives." I walked to the door, not sure what normal would be anymore. I stuck my head into the hallway. Where were Mom and Dad?

"Jack, come here," Bryce called after me. "I want to tell you what happened."

Mom and Dad were in a waiting room across the hall with the doctor. I caught Mom's attention and waved her over. The doctor stopped whatever conversation they were having, and the three of them strode into the room, a small army on a mission.

The doctor spoke first. "Bryce, I'll schedule you for some testing to make sure your brain is healing properly. Your mom and dad can accompany you if they want, but it will be a few hours, so I suggest," he paused and looked at me, "Jack, you go home and get some sleep. Eat a decent meal. Come back tomorrow when we'll know more. You both have gone through quite an experience and need time to recuperate."

I was relieved to go home to Grandpa's and sleep in a real bed. Dad gave Bryce a hug and told him to look after Mom. He squeezed Mom's shoulder on his way out. "Call me if there's any news."

Chapter 34
Bryce

Mom sat beside me on the lumpy hospital bed. A nurse came in with a Jell-O cup and a white plastic water bottle with a bendy straw sticking out of it. I tried some Jell-O, letting it melt in my mouth. It reminded me of eating the strawberries in the mountains, but it wasn't nearly as good. After a few small bites, I set my spoon aside. "Maybe I'll be hungrier later. Thank you, though."

"You're welcome, dear. Get some sleep. I'll come back when it's time to take you down for testing." She smiled at Mom and drew the privacy curtain shut on her way out.

Mom combed through my hair with her slender fingers. "The doctor told me you're doing really well for how long you were unconscious. He said your mental capacity seems to be normal, but he doesn't want to push you too quickly. Plus, you broke three ribs and sprained your ankle pretty badly."

"Oh, yeah. My side hurts when I move. But my headache is worse."

"Has it gotten any better since they gave you medicine for it?" Mom rubbed my head gently.

"A little, I guess." I tilted my head to the side and breathed deeply. "You know, when I fell?"

"Yeah?"

"Something strange happened."

"Oh?" She raised her eyebrows.

"Even though my body was unconscious, I could see myself, and Jack carrying me out of the gorge. It was like . . . like I was hovering above myself for a while."

Mom's fingers stopped moving through my hair.

"I mean, I could see Jack from outside my body. Not with my physical eyes but with something inside me. It's hard to explain. But it was more real than anything I've ever experienced. Not like a dream at all." I tried turning onto my side to face her, but it was too painful. "I guess it was my subconscious seeing Jack, if that's possible. Then I was in some kind of heaven or something. I saw so many things. It's hard to explain." My eyes grew heavy. "I know it seems crazy, but it's true."

Mom squinted and nodded.

I closed my eyes, remembering. "Grandma was there too. She was so beautiful and lit-up, with fiery-red curly hair and the greenest eyes I've ever seen. She made me feel at home and talked to me. I wanted to stay, but she told me it wasn't my time yet. I had to come back and tell all of you she loves you and she's happy. She's waiting for Grandpa. For all of us, I guess." I knew I was rambling, but I had to get it out.

"Wow," said Mom, her eyebrows raised. "I've heard about this kind of thing happening, but . . . that's amazing, Bryce. Let's talk about it more after you get some rest."

I nodded, closing my eyes, and soon fell fast asleep.

Another nurse woke me up later. "Time for your tests," she said in a much-too-excited voice. "I pulled a wheelchair in for you. We don't want you walking just yet."

Still in a daze from being so sound asleep, I couldn't comprehend what she was saying to me. I hadn't even dreamed, though I wished I had. I wanted to catch one more glimpse of Grandma, even if it was only in a dream. Words weren't sufficient to describe it, so maybe a dream could help me figure it out. Five or six senses or even a hundred wouldn't be enough to describe it. There had been so many colors. It reminded me of looking into one of those mega packs of crayons with colors named Mac-n-Cheese or Purple Mountain's Majesty. But no amount of crazy color names would cover the array of light and dark and all the shades in between that I had seen.

The nurse wheeled me through the white halls. The harsh light grated against me, nothing like the warm, liquid, heart-beating light I now knew existed.

While waiting for the tests, I tried reading a magazine but got distracted by every person who walked into the waiting room. One lady had the saddest eyes I'd ever seen—slanted downward, heavy, and filled with pain. What could be so sad to make a person look that way? An impulse to go and hug the woman almost made me get out of my wheelchair and embrace her.

"It's not polite to stare, Bryce," whispered Mom. She followed my gaze and glanced at the lady.

"Oh. Sorry. She looks so sad." I turned my nose down in the magazine.

I couldn't help notice each person who walked in and sense the emotional loads they carried. Physical pain. Anger. Grief. Guilt. I didn't know how I could tell, but I just could. Each one tugged at my heart. When I wasn't watching people, I watched the second hand of the clock tick by. Each second was an instant and, yet, seemed like an eternity. Meaningful and whole, but only a dot in an endless circle. Like when I touched Grandma's fingertips before I left her.

At the end of the day, I was exhausted when they rolled me to my room. A red message light blinked on the telephone. Dad had called to check in. Mom returned his call with a quick, uneventful update. She didn't tell him what I'd said about being in heaven though.

Mom hung up the phone. "Dad said Jack slept all day, woke up, ate most of what was in the house, and went to bed again."

"Sounds like him." I chuckled.

"I'll go find us some food. What do you feel like eating?" she asked.

"Maybe some Jell-O, but I'm really sleepy."

The nurse helped me into bed. Mom adjusted my pillows and turned down the lights. I soon fell asleep again.

Chapter 35
Bryce

The next morning at ten, Dad and Jack arrived at the hospital while I was eating toast and a banana. I smiled at them. "Hi, Dad! How's it going? Feeling better, Jack?" I asked, feeling cheerful.

Mom raised her eyebrows and smirked at Dad.

Dad bent down, hugging me awkwardly. "Glad to see you up and at 'em." He ruffled my hair and wiped his hand on his jeans. "Maybe you'll get to take a shower today."

"After being cramped in this bed, a shower would feel great." I pushed away the tray holding the remains of my picked-over breakfast.

"How are you?" Jack smiled.

"Better than you by the looks of it," I joked, and held up my hand for a fist bump. Jack reached over to meet me halfway from the chair he sat in.

"Where's Grandpa?" I asked.

Dad answered, "He's getting coffee for Mom, and then he'll be up."

"Oh, okay. I guess I can tell him later then."

"Tell him what?" asked Dad.

"About what happened to me when I fell."

Mom and Dad sat down on the cot. Jack crossed his arms and legs.

"What do you mean?" asked Dad.

"I've been thinking about the best way to explain it." I cleared my throat and sipped some water. "I know this is going to sound crazy, but just listen. When I fell, I was unconscious, right? At least my body was, but I could see my body lying there, close to the river. I could see Jack and hear him trying to wake me up."

Their wide eyes watched me, unblinking. I could guess what they were thinking. I sighed heavily. "What I mean is, the deepest part of me"—I pointed to my chest—"I guess it would be my subconscious or my soul, was still alert. I could see Jack reviving my body and carrying me to the cabin. I couldn't understand why he was so worried though, because I was fine. There's another world around us. In us, even. I wanted to stay there forever. It was hard coming back." I looked past all of them, remembering.

Dad interrupted me and quietly asked, "Are you joking?"

Jack jumped in. "I told him it was a vivid dream."

"Yeah, it had to be a dream," Dad said. "You were probably at least somewhat aware of what was happening around you. The doctors say that can happen. I'm sure you heard Jack taking care of you. You knew what was going on and dreamed it."

Mom laid her hand on Dad's arm. "Why don't we let Bryce finish."

Dad huffed, and Jack protested, "We can't let him believe what he's saying is true."

Mom sounded firm. "I think we need to respect your brother and his experience and show him how grateful we are to have him with us safe and sound."

Jack slouched in his chair and pressed his lips together.

As I rehashed the details of my journey, Jack said, "I can't believe you're feeding us these lies or whatever they are, and we're supposed to pretend to believe them. This is ridiculous!"

"Jack, just listen," I begged. "Grandma was there. She gave me a message to tell you."

"What?" Jack palmed his forehead. "You've got to be joking."

"Jack, settle down," commanded Mom.

Grandpa came in the room then, reading the various expressions on our faces. Mom's—worried. Dad's—shocked. Jack's—livid. I could guess at the look on my own face—pleading for them to listen and understand me.

I tried again. It was so much easier talking to Grandpa. But that's when it hit me. I still had a secret I was keeping from him. I wondered where the map and pictures had ended up. I'd have to tell him the whole truth if I expected him to believe any of it. My stomach clenched.

"Grandpa, I'm trying to tell them about my fall, but I have to back up and tell you what happened before that." I recalled the whole story about me finding the pictures, and map, and then the tree with the engraving in it.

"And I found a box buried beneath the tree . . ."

Mom gasped and it seemed like the air in the room got thicker. Her chin started to quiver. Dad's face got all red. He looked like he was about to explode. I couldn't understand why everyone was getting so upset. What I'd done was wrong, but it wasn't *that* bad.

"I wish you would've told me the truth," Grandpa said, the lines on his face sagging. "I do understand. I know how lies and secrets can get away from us. It happens fast." He looked at Mom and Dad. "But you should know you can tell me anything. Anytime."

"I know. I'm so sorry I lied to you. And stole from you." I hung my head. "I hope you can forgive me someday."

Grandpa leaned down and hugged me gently. "Of course, I forgive you. I love you."

I swallowed, thankful for the best grandpa in the world. Not sure how to read Mom and Dad's exchanged glances and pained expressions, I continued. "I know it's hard to believe, but I really was with Grandma. She was alive and so beautiful. She talked to me even."

"Oh?" Grandpa sat on the edge of the bed.

Mom added quietly, "He described her hair and eyes perfectly."

Grandpa tipped his head toward me. "She was a rare beauty." He smiled a bittersweet smile and sighed.

"I wanted to stay with her, but she said I had to tell you that she loves you and misses you. She's happy, and she wants you to be happy too." I nodded at Grandpa. "And that you're not to blame. She said to be sure to tell you that you are not to blame. But I didn't know what she was talking about."

Grandpa breathed deeply, and his eyes glistened. A thin trail of a tear rolled down his cheek. I had caught a glimpse of how much Grandma missed him, so I could guess at how Grandpa missed her too.

"She died suddenly from a heart attack," Grandpa said. "I've always felt like it was my fault because I went fishing that day. I should have been there for her."

Everyone was silent. Grandpa wiped his nose and asked, "You really did see her, you say?"

"Yes, sir, I did." I nodded solemnly.

Grandpa looked out the window and stared for a long moment, maybe trying to see her too.

Chapter 36

Bryce

Dad rested his forehead in his hands and shook his head.

Jack sat with his fists clenched in his lap.

I didn't know how else to convince them. Maybe Mom could help me persuade them. Despite their doubtful looks, I continued. "I wanted to hug Grandma, but I couldn't. She was holding a baby on her lap. He was beautiful. Perfect. She was taking care of him, and they were waiting for us."

Mom's eyes widened and she sucked in a deep breath.

"Grandma said his name was William, the same name I found carved into the tree by the lake. It had the year 2002 too, so I wondered . . ."

A sudden hush came over the room, as if a vacuum had sucked all the air out. Their eyes flashed at me.

"What? What did I say?" I asked, scanning their faces.

"How dare you!" accused Dad. "Enough of this!" He jumped up.

Mom rubbed the palms of her hands across her eyes like she was trying to stop tears from falling. "Marcus, please." She tugged his arm and held one hand over her heart like she'd been shot.

"Who is William?" Jack looked around for answers. "Bryce asked me about him just before he fell."

I continued. "He was important to Grandma. And he seemed familiar to me." I looked at Jack and cocked my head. The baby reminded me of Jack, now that I thought about it.

Mom shuffled to the side of the bed, faced all of us, and hugged her shoulders. "William is . . . was . . ." She slumped, broken down and suddenly much older than I had realized. "William is our son."

Jack and I studied Mom and then each other. The information settled on us like dust from an explosion.

"Like a stepson?" I asked.

Mom shook her head slowly and pressed her lips together.

"So . . . what you're telling us is . . . what?" Jack spoke one word at a time, trying to comprehend.

A nurse walked into the room and my entire family tensed.

"A few more minutes of privacy, please," Dad requested. She turned abruptly and left.

"Andrea," Dad said, "you don't have to do this."

"Yes, I do." She nodded and sighed heavily. "Yes, I

do. It's been a long time coming. I should have known—secrets always have a way of coming out, don't they?" She squinted at me.

I nodded. "Tell us, Mom. What is it? What happened to Will?"

"Will is your brother, Bryce. And your brother, Jack." With a trenched brow she searched his eyes—or maybe she was searching for the right words. "He was your identical twin brother, Jack, just a few minutes older than you. He died in his crib almost three months after the two of you were born. They said it was SIDS."

Jack must have stopped breathing. He didn't move or make a sound for several seconds. Then he jumped up from his chair, looking like someone had kicked him in the gut. "I lost a twin brother? And you never told me? Why didn't you ever tell me?" he pleaded.

Mom and Dad were silent.

"You've both lied to me my whole life?" He shot them a harsh, accusing look. "I . . . I just . . . don't . . ." He rushed past Mom. She reached her trembling fingers out to him, but he brushed her off and left the room without a word.

Dad shot up after him, but Grandpa put a restraining hand on his arm. Grandpa leaned over and squeezed my shoulder before leaving the room. "I'll go talk to him."

An uncomfortable silence hung between us, and I asked, "What's SIDS, Mom?"

She stared out the door after Jack with her hand to her mouth.

A moment later, Dad answered for her, "It stands for Sudden Infant Death Syndrome. In most cases, like with Will, they don't really know why the baby dies. We woke up one morning and he was . . . gone." His voice cracked.

Mom's normal calmness fell and was replaced with tears swelling her eyes. She reached for a tissue beside my bed. By the time she turned back toward Dad, her shoulders were shaking with silent sobs. Dad stood and wrapped her in his arms as she blew her nose. It was the first time in a long time I'd seen them hug. Now I could see why they'd always been so sad. They'd held their pain in for fourteen years. Pain for a son they'd never gotten to read their favorite books to or teach to ride a bike. Pain for a brother we'd never get to play football with or challenge in an Xbox tournament.

I watched my parents' rare warmhearted moment and had an urge to break in between them. To be a part of it. If I weren't stuck in the bed, I probably would have.

The nurse spoiled the moment by checking my vitals. Mom and Dad moved apart but stayed connected, holding hands.

"We need to find Jack." Dad looked at Mom for a long moment like he was seeing her in a different way. He looked back at me. "We'll be right back."

Twenty minutes later, Mom, Dad, and Grandpa walked back into the room with Jack straggling behind them. His eyes were red and puffy. I was shocked. I'd never seen him cry before. He sank into the chair and looked very small, as if the wind had been deflated out of him.

Dad broke the silence. "When Will died, our hearts broke. But we had to cope the best we could because we still had you, Jack, and we loved you . . . we love you so much." Jack sat still, staring down at his knees.

I was shocked to hear Dad speak of loving Jack. I didn't think I'd ever heard him say that before.

Dad continued. "But the pain of losing Will hung on for a long time. It still hurts if I let myself think about it."

Mom wiped her eyes again, blew her nose, and continued the story. "Bryce, when you were born, Jack was almost three. We were thrilled. It was like you'd be the brother Jack lost. But there never was a good time to tell either of you about Will. It was such an unbearable pain that I hid from most people. Even from myself, most of the time. It's also why we moved away from Colorado then. I couldn't face rehashing the pain with our friends here."

"We swore Grandpa and Grandma and the rest of our family to secrecy. It was our secret to tell you when the time was right. And I couldn't handle talking to anyone about it, least of all telling my two darling little boys that their baby brother had died. I've always felt like . . . like Will's death was my fault. Like I did something wrong that last night when I kissed his soft, chubby cheeks and laid him to sleep in his crib."

Dad pulled Mom close. Jack and I looked away and then at each other. A deep, tense pain wavered in his watery eyes. I could only imagine the hurt, anger, or maybe betrayal he was feeling. It started to make sense—why we had never gotten along and why he had always seemed so lost and alone. Even depressed. There was a big part of Jack that was missing. And he had never known about it.

I couldn't fill the hole, even if I had been the perfect brother. I wondered how different Jack might be today if Will hadn't died. And how different we all would be.

As we stared at each other, I could see Jack's countenance change. Maybe imperceptibly at first, but it was a start. A new beginning for him . . . for all of us.

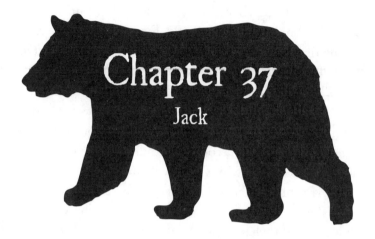

Chapter 37

Jack

Looking back on that day, a darkness I'd always felt began to lift off me, replaced by a dawn of relief, rising slow and steady, like a sunrise. I always felt like I wasn't good enough for Mom and Dad. I never understood why, of course, and I resented them for it.

In a way, it was true—I never could be good enough for them. There was a huge piece missing from their lives. No matter what I did, I would never be able to fill the hole left in them from Will's absence. It was a Will-shaped hole. And I was Jack-shaped.

Now, I understood why I always felt Mom's sadness around me. She loved me, of course, like a mother loves her child, but I must have always reminded her of Will. What he would have been like when he was two and toddling around, or how he would have grown up into a teenager. Will would've been different than me, of course, but I would've been different too. If Will was still here, we would've had each other, and all these holes never would've existed.

I didn't know the emptiness in me was from a brother I never knew. Well, maybe not never. I guess I did know him better than anyone else until we were almost three months old.

And maybe I did still know him. If Bryce really was in heaven, and Will was there, then maybe he was still a part of me.

Mom and Dad cleared their schedules for the rest of the month so we could spend time all together as a family with Grandpa. They even hiked up to the cabin for a couple of days, and retrieved the treasure, and the things Jack had left behind. They said they needed to revisit Will and spend some time, just the two of them, working through some things. They confessed to us that they'd had divorce papers written up while we were on vacation, but now, things were changing between them, between all of us.

When Bryce was all better, I took him to 7-Eleven to get that Slurpee I'd promised him. As we walked back to home, I had a thought as we passed a big pharmacy. "Let's stop in here." The store was filled with gifts, toys, tools, and all sorts of things. I looked through the aisles for a journal, wanting to start writing in one like Grandpa had. Maybe I'd be able to sort out everything that had happened on the trip and figure out what I wanted to do with my life. Since the helicopter ride, I was interested in what it would take to get into search and rescue. The way Mike had saved Bryce's life inspired me to want to help others like that.

Inside the store, on a shelf of office supplies, I found a small black notebook that would work as a journal and showed Bryce.

"What's that for?" he asked.

I shrugged. "I've got some thinking to do. Thought I'd try writing about it."

"Cool," he said as we made our way to the checkout line.

I handed the notebook to the cashier.

"This it?" the man asked.

I nodded, but then Bryce bopped me on the shoulder and said, "Hang on." He ran back and disappeared down an aisle.

"What is it?" I called out.

A moment later, he jogged back with a football in his hand and handed it and his ten-dollar bill he got from doing chores to the cashier.

"Maybe I can help you practice," Bryce said with a grin, "so you can make starting quarterback this year."

I couldn't help but smile. I was sure that's exactly what Will would have done if he were here. Maybe Bryce and I could figure this friendship thing out after all.

All the way back home, Bryce ran ahead of me along the street as I lofted pass after pass into his arms.

Acknowledgments

First, I thank God, who is always with me.

This book never would have been written if not for a lifetime of adventure and undying support given to me by my parents, Jerry and Judy Williams. Nor would it have been written if my dear friend Jenda Nye hadn't been there from page one, telling me to write a book, critiquing it for me, and believing in me. Now it's your turn, girl!

I owe so much to the online writing community on Twitter: Brenda Drake (for #PitMad, through which I received so much agent feedback), Jessica Schmeidler (for her pitch workshop and #JustPitchIt, which led me to my first R&Rs), and Jessica Sinsheimer, whose #MSWL led me to finding the perfect home for this book. I'm also grateful to the community on Critique Circle where many of my critique partners were anonymous and gave copious feedback. I wish I could thank each one of them personally. But I did get to know Sally Hughes Doherty, who, very generously, stuck with me through the whole book and helped me see my story through fresh eyes.

My critique partners are the most generous people! Sarah Floyd, you encouraged me and talked me down from The Ledge when I wasn't sure if I could do it. Emily

Moore, you're a genius brainstormer and editor and a sweet friend. Melyssa Mercado and Michelle Hulse, you both enthusiastically helped me refine my opening pages and premise. Marissa Fuller and Lisa Jane Weller, thank you for starting me out on the right path with generous R&Rs. And to every single one of my 100 agent or editor rejections: Rejection stings, but it pushed me toward becoming a better writer and telling a deeper story.

Thank you, Alistair Dunnington, for your amazing illustrations in the book and for filming and producing the trailer. In both, you were able to capture what I envisioned and more. Thank you, Joshua Schwarz and Zachary Schwarz, for being the perfect Jack and Bryce in the trailer.

I'm so grateful to my acquiring editor, Ashley Gephart, at Cedar Fort, who saw the value of my story and took me through the most amazing editing experience I've ever had. Thank you, E. B. Wheeler, fellow Cedar Fort author, for helping me navigate the whole publishing experience. Michelle May Ledezma, I think of you every time I look at my cover, which I love. And Justin Greer, thank you for painstakingly going through my book. The whole staff at Cedar Fort has made my lifelong dream come true in such a positive way!

And, to save the best for last . . . I wrote this story for my boys: Josh, Zach, Evan, and Ben. Thank you for reading my book, helping me revise it, cheering me on, and giving me time and space to do this. And to Christian . . . there's no one in the world I'd rather be with on this great adventure than you.

About the Author

Shari loves reading or writing a good adventure story as much as she loves hiking in the Colorado mountains. No matter where life has taken her, be it the Philippines, coaching gymnastics, or working as a school librarian, she has always returned to writing stories, poetry, or blogging at www.sharischwarz.com.

Though she'll forever be a Colorado girl at heart, where she lives with her husband and their four boys, she relishes long walks on foggy Oregon-coast beaches with a latte in hand. When she's not working on her latest adventure story, you can find her gardening, hiking, or spinning awkward dance moves in her kitchen.